D1030868

The Lost and the Lurking

The Lost
and the Lurking

MANLY WADE WELLMAN

DOUBLEDAY & COMPANY, INC.

GARDEN CITY, NEW YORK

1981

All of the characters in this book
are fictitious, and any resemblance
to actual persons, living or dead,
is purely coincidental.

Library of Congress Cataloging in Publication Data

Wellman, Manly Wade, 1905–
    The lost and the lurking.

    I. Title.
PS3545.E52858L6   813'.54
AACR2
ISBN: 0-385-17155-2
Library of Congress Catalog Card Number 81–65662

First Edition

for
Kirby McCauley
who got me to write it

Horatio: O day and night, but this is wondrous strange!
Hamlet: And therefore as a stranger give it welcome.
    —*Hamlet, Prince of Denmark,* ACT I, SCENE 5

The Lost and the Lurking

CHAPTER 1

I'd been told to look out for three trees on the west side of
the highway, three tall tulip poplars bunched up like a green
bouquet for some big giant girl. When I saw them ahead, I
asked the bus driver to stop and let me off. He did that thing
and then drove on away round a curve, a-leaving me where
there was no house in sight, with my backpack and my silver-
strung guitar. I reckoned it to be maybe on to four o'clock in
the evening.

Both ways from those three poplars grew thick, brushy
willow and laurel scrub. Far off through their branches I saw
the mountains lift to the west, dim and gray-green as clouds.
A sign had been put up beside the road, THIS PROPERTY FOR
SALE, but it had fallen off its post and most likely nobody had
made air offer to buy. It was harder to find another sign next
the highest poplar. A lean, slaty rock there, tall as up to my
tall shoulder, and, chopped into it, one letter atop of another:

W
O
L
V
E
R
3 MILES

Wolver. That put me in mind of a mountain called
Wolter, where once I'd spent a right rough night with a cou-

ple of Druids who got themselves struck dead by lightning and were better off dead thattaway. So here I was, more or less on the eastern slope of the Appalachians—never mind right exactly where, that's maybe still an official secret. You could barely see the way through, hardly enough of one to be named a road. It sneaked through the brush a little bit past the three poplars. I hiked up my stuff and headed in along it.

No great much of a road, gentlemen, and no great much traveled. Just two pebbly-graveled ruts with grass grown up betwixt them, but I traveled it because the government wanted me to. The thing had begun when a Washington man followed me along to where I was to make some music for a wedding party at Sky Notch at the foot of Dogged Mountain. He allowed he'd come from the White House itself, with a duty for me to do. The President of the United States called upon me personally, and well you know that when the President of the United States calls upon you, you hark at him. You do his bidding.

"John," the government man had said, "we want you to go to a little place called Wolver, and find out exactly what's happening there." Not that he was much able to give me a notion. He only kept on a-talking about how the government knew that I'd been into some strange doings in my time, that I had some knowledge and maybe some power. "All we can certainly say," he'd added on to that, "is that there's no legal operation there in a position to give you any help. But things seem to be uncanny, and things might grow to be dangerous. Dangerous to the people of this country." He'd said more like that, but not much of it what you'd call helpful. I got it in mind that, whatever went on in Wolver, it was reckoned to be dead wrong, and it was up to me to find out if I could and make a report back to the people in Washington. So there by God I was, a-walking along the rutted road, with my pack on my back and my old guitar under my arm. And what

I was set to look for at Wolver I didn't rightly know, though maybe I suspicioned a thing or two.

I got past the trees that grew at the highway, and then I could see out across thickets and clumps to the mountains way off yonder. They weren't mountains that I much knew; this part of the country was more or less strange to me. And the sky overhead, that was somehow strange. I'd thought it was a clear sky when I was on the bus, but now it had a dull, hot look, like as if there was the least bit of a skin of haze on it. The sun, that worked its way along toward those western mountains was hot, too, but it was made reddish by the haze. I wondered myself if that meant weather a-coming on, rain.

The dirt track curved off to the right up ahead of me, and here and there on the left the ground looked to be cleared. Farm land? But, as I slogged the way on my long legs, I saw that it wasn't. The space was given over to an almighty big trash dump. I made out pits full of dark stuff, and stacks of rubbish, and here and there the old rusty dead bodies of automobiles. One place another, there burned smoky fires. It was what might could have been fair land once, but now all given over to the rot and clutter of what we like to call civilization.

Well, anyway, folks came in this far from off the highway to get shed of the mess they didn't want to keep at home. And what worse mess would be a-waiting for me at Wolver?

I kept on a-making my way past all that jumble and clutter. It was hot, as I've said, and I was a-getting up a sweat. Overhead the sun shone, blurred and brick red, and the dull sky wasn't exactly clouded. I wondered how came it to be so. On I came to where, just clear of the trash dump and set back from the side of the road under some trees of different kinds, I saw a little house. It was no more than a cabin, made of planks up and down like a tobacco barn. A man came out at the door of it. A black man, I could half see, half guess, at the distance. He wasn't much more than only middling big, but he moved like somebody with some muscle on his bones. I flung up a hand at him and he flung one up at me, good-mannered country style. My old boots stirred up the gravel in a stretch of the rut I walked on. I looked to be the only traffic on the move along that road.

The trees grew in close round a stretch of the way there, thick, dark-leafed trees, with a sort of swampy look to them. They hugged in both sides till you'd think air kind of good-sized car would rattle their twigs to right and left. Their branches grew together overhead like a roof, and made it twilighty under them. I had me a notion that some of those branches were like trailing arms, and their twigs like clawed fingers. As I walked along under them, I wondered myself didn't I hear whispery voices, though that might could have been a little puff of breeze somewhere deep in yonder. And, when I looked while I walked, sparks of light winked and stirred in the shadows. Here and there winked two sparks together, like eyes a-looking out at me. I picked up my feet to make it faster through that creepy wooded stretch to where it opened out and I could see the country.

By that time, I was a good bit better than a couple miles in from where I'd got off the bus, and I reckoned I should ought to be soon a-coming to that place called Wolver. I didn't expect to be much worried about, just a-walking in thattaway. Sure I was a man some taller than the average, but not enough to pester somebody a-meeting up with me. Old hat, old shirt, old jeans pants, old boots, my bundle and my guitar. Just possibly, the guitar would get me a welcome. It had done that thing for me in a many strange places. If it did that for me now, if it got folks till they'd talk to me, I'd be where I could more or less likely figure out about what the government wanted me to learn and bring back on doings in Wolver.

And now I'd reached to where there was thickety woods on

just my left and, on my right, open ground again and a church house, with the dull, hot sky hung over it.

It had been well built once, that church house, but it had gone all shackily and a dark, paint-hungry gray on its plank walls. The steeple was cocked over to one side, near about ready to fall, the old wooden shingles of the roof sort of ruffled up like a hen's feathers, air windowpane I could see busted in. I doubted myself if the good word was preached there these days. The yard was shagged over with weeds and scrub, in amongst which showed old gravestones. Naught looks worse and lonelier than a church house where folks have quit their worship. I walked my way past, and right soon I came to one end of what had to be the main street of Wolver, though no street sign showed.

The dirt road smoothed and widened out, it had been used quite a bit to make it into a street. Along both sides were spaced out houses, fairly far apart, near about as unchancy-looking as houses might could be expected to look. And, gentlemen, in my time I've seen some right unchancy-looking ones.

They were cabin built, mostly, of squared poles with white-washed clay chinking, and one or two were of boards set straight up and down on end, the way the cabin by the trash dump was made. The windows looked secret, with drapes inside them. The yards were fenced in with low rows of poles laid crosswise, and the grass all tromped down inside them. In one yard I thought I saw a dog, middling-sized and black. But when it cocked its head to look at me, were those horns on its head? A goat, then; only no goat would have such long upstanding ears like a mule, such a pushed-in face, almost like a monkey's. In another yard, some children were a-playing, or anyhow sitting up together close. They looked at me, too, and they had pale, squinchy faces, like mean old men and women.

Next to the yard with the children, a man stood on the doorlog of his house, a-holding what looked to be a dark-covered book open against his chest. He wore brown clothes, homemade as I figured. I put up a hand and called out "hidy" to him, but he turned away and cut his eyes sidelong at me, and then quick went back in. No friendly manners there. I recollected a song I'd heard years back, sung I think by Burl Ives, about "A stranger in town, where a stranger ain't welcome." Would it be like that here? A-humming the song to myself, I could see I'd come more or less to what was the middle of Wolver.

A trail cut across the main street there, not more than a footpath really, with a few houses strung out to right and left on it. At the right corner of this crossing, the one nearest to me, rose up what was far and away the biggest dwelling house in the whole place. It was masked in with cedar trees, grown as close as a hedge, but I could see pillars in front and white-painted stone walls and an upper story, with a flat roof to it. Catty-corner across from that place, other side of the street, was what looked to be a country store of gray-weathered clapboards, with a porch all the way across and people on the porch. Then more houses the rest of the way along the street, to where showed another big building, old red brick with blue-painted windows, like a mill of some kind.

All right, I'd got to where I was to be. Where could I fling my gear down? I decided to try that big house as I came near. I turned in at a gateway set amongst the cedars—it had two big brick posts to the sides, and a sort of twisty iron bar at the top—and then along a path flagged with slate stones, with droopy-looking white and yellow flowers to both its edges. I stepped up on a porch floored with square stone chunks of different colors, and swung on the brass knocker that was made of a ring in the jaws of a sort of monkey face.

I waited. Nair sound inside the heavy, nail-patterned white planks of the door. Again I knocked and again I waited.

Windows were set to each side, little, colored-glass windows. I had the notion that somebody or something looked out at me. Then, finally, the door opened, with a sort of twang of its hinges.

A man stood there, near about little enough to be called a dwarf. Well, maybe a couple inches under five feet. He was skinny-shouldered and scrawny-legged, in the gray store suit he wore with a green shirt and a green string tie. His hair was balded off in front, and at the sides it was so dull-colored you couldn't rightly say was it brown or gray. He had a nose as thin and sharp as half a pair of shears, and blinky green eyes, and a mouth that looked to wonder itself whether to pout or giggle.

"Yes?" he said, and his voice was high and scrapy. "Yes, what is it?"

In past him, the house looked chuck full of shadows. I got a kind of hint that there was something just behind him, some sort of crouching animal, shiny-black and quiet.

"I'm sorry to pester you like this, sir," I said, "but I was a-walking through, and it's a-coming on late in the evening before sundown. So I wondered if there might could be some place—a rooming house, maybe—where I could get to stay all night."

"Stay all night?" he scraped out the words after me. "Who are you?"

And he might as well have put it, Who the hell are you?

"My name's John," I said, and felt glad just then that it wasn't a scarced-out name to say. "I'm just a-making my way through this part of the country—"

"Sorry, John," he broke in on me, and not sorry a bit. "There are no rooming houses here in Wolver. Nothing of that description whatever. You'll have to go somewhere else."

With that, he slammed the door on me, another sight harder than I'd reckoned such a little scrap of a fellow could slam it.

"A stranger in town, where a stranger ain't welcome," I hummed to myself one more time. Well, if there wasn't a roof to go over me in Wolver, I'd manage without one. I'd done that over the years, often. But I'd better have me some rations. So I walked across to the store.

Up above the porch, a homemade plank sign said EULA JARBOE. There were five–six men on the porch, and one girl. She sat on a bench against the front, a small, nice-shaped girl with fluffy blond hair and a home-sewn dress of some kind of checked cloth. She watched me with blue eyes, like as if I was the strangest-looking animal she'd air seen in all her born days. The men watched me, too. They sat or lounged round, different sizes and ages, mostly a-wearing brown clothes that looked homemade, too. I didn't see friendship in one eye amongst the whole bunch.

"Hidy," I said, and there, too, nobody replied me. I went in past them, through the open door into the place.

It was more or less like all other country store houses. The walls were planks, without a lick of paint to show on them or the rafters, nor yet on the shelves or the rough-built counter. I saw some old-fashioned barrels in a row, and against the wall were hung some home-smoked hams and shoulders and bacon flitches. Back of the counter, beside an inner door, stood a stout-built woman with gray in her darkish hair and eyes so bright they sort of bit at you.

"Yes?" she said, and she didn't sound much like as if she meant yes to aught I had to say.

"I'm a-walking on through, ma'am," I replied her, and dropped my gear beside the counter. "I just reckoned on buying a few things to eat."

"I'll sell you what you may want," she said, in a voice to mean she would be a-doing me a big favor.

The blond-haired girl had walked into the place behind me as I looked here and yonder for what I might take. I asked for a few rashers of bacon, and the storekeeper woman took a big sharp knife and slit them off the flitch for me and wrapped them up. I inquired her might I have a little poke of corn-meal, and with a scoop she took some from one of the barrels. Then a couple tins of sardines and some coffee, and from a big wheel of yellow cheese a hunk. I paid for the things with some of the expense money I'd been given. Then I turned round and shoved them into the soogin sack I carried along with my rolled-up blanket. And that's when I saw that my guitar had left out of there, somehow.

Right away quick, I headed back out onto the porch. Sure enough, that girl had sat down on the bench, my silver-strung guitar in her hands, one pink finger a-jangling it.

"Excuse me, miss," I said, stepping to her, "you've got my guitar."

"I ain't about to hurt it," she said, a-turning her blue eyes up to me.

"Nobody touches it but just me myself," I told her, and took the guitar out of her hands.

She jumped up off the bench and sort of scurried away. All those five–six men stood up and turned their eyes on me.

CHAPTER 2

I stood by the bench with my guitar in my hand and I saw them plain, the half dozen of them, for the first time.

All sizes, big and little, and different ages. Yet there was something alike in their faces; a sort of blank look to each and all of those faces, their eyes wided out, their mouths loose; blank, and at the same time as mean and poisonous as that many snakes.

"Well," said the biggest one, and he was sort of soft and porky to the look, with clumsy-made gray bib overalls and his hair roan-red and balded at the top. "Well, well, well," he said, "it seems to me like as if you're right careful of that there old guitar not to have it out of your hands."

"You're right about that, friend," I said back to him. "That's just how I am about it."

"You didn't have no call whatever to talk like that to Lute Baynor, she wasn't about to hurt that old box of yours," he sort of blustered at me.

So that was her name, Lute Baynor. She stood at the door of the store house, sort of a-glittering her blue eyes at me, excited by the way all those men had taken up for her.

"She won't hurt it if I can help it," I said. "Nobody will."

None of them liked that, not one bit. They churned their faces into scowls.

"Now, then," said one of the others, "what if we all of us had a look at it, sort of passed it round amongst us?"

With that, the whole scowling bunch came forward a step or so, a-bunching up. I didn't relish the notion of fighting all of them at once, and wondered if I couldn't fix it to fight just one. I chose out the big, porky man.

"You're the biggest of your bunch," I said to him. "Are you the best? Maybe you and I can try it on for two–three minutes."

And I laid my guitar down on top of my blanket and bag, and sort of set my feet how they'd best be set.

"Hold on," said a deep, hard voice from down in the yard.

A man came fast walking across from the place next door. I had my first look there, and saw it had a shed with a forge in it. The man who came was big, too, but not soft. He wore a short-sleeved blue shirt and over his belly a leather apron. His hair was scaldy-pale yellow, and his face was as square as the bottom of a cracker box. He looked all humpy with muscle. He stepped up on the porch, and the others pulled back to let him come.

"If there's aught of fighting to be done here," he allowed, "I'll do it. I always do."

I reckoned he'd be harder to mess with than old tallow-pudgy, but I faced him. He looked me all up and down, like as if he was a-seeing where would be a good place to hit me.

"What name do you go by?" he inquired me.

"John."

He snorted through wide nostrils. "What's the rest of your name?"

"John's enough for you."

"Huh, John," he repeated me. "My name's Ottom Orcutt, and I ain't scared to give all of it. I been a-hearing lots of debate from where I was at work, so let's give off the talk and have the action. John, if that's your true name, we don't much see strangers here, and when we do, we like them to act right."

"I don't reckon I've acted other than right, Mr. Orcutt," I said. "What I told them was, I don't relish folks a-fooling with my guitar."

"That there old thing?" he said, and made a step like as if he was about to pick it up.

I figured I'd better hit him right then and there, and I did, hard on the side of his big, thick jaw. He stepped back and blinked, and I hit him again and chopped his lip open, and then we were at it.

I told myself he'd better not get set to punch as hard as he could, and I ducked down to let what he meant for my chin just scrape my hairline, but even then it shook me. I got both my fists, one after the other, into his big hard belly, and got them in again, four good half-arm digs that made him grunt. I could hear the others all a-hollering and a-bellowing with, "Hit him, Ottom!" and "Let him have it!" but I was able not to let that happen.

I was another sight faster on my feet than big, beefy Ottom Orcutt, and I made him miss, which can tire a fellow out. He came a-charging at a run and I sidestepped and fetched him a right smack under the ear that teetered him. When he spun around, his feet were close together for a second and I slipped in close and laid in my fists as fast and often as I could; head and body and head again, maybe eight or ten times in four or five seconds. When he staggered back because he had to, I brought one up, rockabye, so hard I cut my knuckles on the bone of his chin. I speared him again in the middle of the face as he went over backward and hit on the boards of the porch with a slam like a log a-falling off the tail of a truck.

He didn't move where he lay sprawled out, and nair soul spoke for a moment. Then, from the doorway beside Lute Baynor, the storekeeper lady said, "Well, I'll be," like as if she'd nair seen the like in all her born days.

"Get up, Ottom, get up!" they hollered him, but he didn't. He just turned over on his side, slow, and said a cuss word out of the corner of his bloody mouth.

The tallow-pudgy man looked mean at me. "Let's get after

him, boys," he said, but they didn't close in, they only rocked
a moment on their toes and gopped at me.

"Get that guitar, he's away from it," said one of them.

"None of you dares come near it," I said, and I stepped
back to guard it where it lay.

"No," said Ottom Orcutt in a thick voice, and he sat up
and dabbed at his face with his big, meaty hand. "Don't
none of you fuss with it, or him neither."

They backed off from me at his word, and looked at him
and at me and at him again while he got up on his feet, slow
and shaky.

"John," he said, "you sure enough fetched me a good one
then. I nair seen it a-coming. You poured it on me."

"I did it the gentlest I could, Mr. Orcutt," I said. "I hope
you're all right."

"Sure I'm all right," he said, deep and sour. "Just got myself licked fair and square, that's all."

He mopped at his cut mouth again, and looked round at
the others, with eyes set deep and narrow in his bloody face.

"Don't none of you be so weak-minded as to get on John
and try to finish up what I couldn't. I'd warrant that he'd
help you right off again."

"Mr. Orcutt," I said, "I do hope you and I can be friends
now."

"Friends?" he repeated after me, like as if it was a strange
word to him. "Friends? Hell, John, I take me a time to be
friends with somebody. Let's just say me and you fought and
you whipped, and it was a good fight, and let it stand at
that."

I hadn't put out my hand to him to shake, nor neither had
he put his out to me. Air soul was a-listening the way you'd
reckon they'd been paid to listen. The Lute Baynor girl kept
a-studying me and she moved her pink lips without air talk to
come out. Then another voice, from down in the yard. I
looked round thattaway.

It was the little skinny-shouldered man who'd turned me away from the door of the big house.

"Sir," he said. "John. Will you come with me? Tiphaine says she'd like a word with you."

"Sure enough," I said, and picked up the guitar and the blanket roll and soogin sack. "Good day, Mr. Orcutt. Good day, ladies and gentlemen."

Air soul pulled way back off and stared as I went down the step from the porch to where the little man waited.

"My name's Quill Norbury," he made himself known, and gave me his hand, not much bigger than a chicken foot and sort of wettish cold. "As I said, Tiphaine wants to talk with you. Come along this way."

We headed back across the street to the big house with its hedge of cedar, and I felt all those eyes a-staring at my back as we went. And over all things, that dull sky, that blurred, hot sun.

Again in at that gate with the iron thing across the top, and again along the path through the shrubby yard with the pale flowers that sort of stared at you. Quill Norbury opened the door and led me in and we stopped in the hall.

"Wait here, will you," he said, and trotted on away to a sort of gloomy inner door and opened it and was out of my sight.

I had time as I stood alone to see that the hall was long and narrow and high up, with stairs along one side, and brown-stained wood walls, what they call paneling. On the floor I saw what I'd seen earlier, what looked like an animal hunkered down there. It was what you might call a statue, of dark, shiny stone, and its body was more or less of a wildcat, but the front was a woman. Quite a lot of woman, too, big-bosomed and chubby-shouldered, with hands up and one a-holding a wiggly stone snake and the other what must be a cup or glass. The eyes were gouged-out holes and the mouth a slit chopped in with a chisel, and on the head two horns. Or maybe they were just some kind of hat she wore. Anyway, horns, kinked inward at the points like the horns of a cow.

If that's what they set up here, I said to myself, it might could make a point on the trail I had come to figure out.

Then the inner door opened again.

"Your name is John, they tell me," said a low voice with music in it. "I'm Tiphaine."

My first notion of her was height—she was taller for a woman than I am for a man—and a body that could move easy, move sweet. She had flowing black hair, as shiny as the wing of a grackle. It fell like two thick clouds on her shoulders. She looked at me with bright lamps of eyes, with long lashes that swept to her cheeks when she lowered the lids. Her red lips were full, like sweet, ripe fruits. She wore a sort of drapey gown of dark blue, that didn't make air secret of the fact that she had a figure both full and fine. Gentlemen, she was the best-looking woman you could hope to see in a thousand miles of travel on this earth, and well she knew it.

"I watched your fight with Ottom Orcutt," she said in her sweet, musical voice. "Watched from the front window. I don't understand how you beat him so badly, John. He's twice as big as you are."

"Not quite that much bigger, ma'am," I said.

"In any case, he's generally supposed to put his knuckles where they do the most damage."

"He laid a knuckle to me only the one time," I said, and I tried not to sound like a brag. "It got me high up on the head, I wasn't hurt to matter, ma'am."

"Just call me Tiphaine. But Ottom—well, he's supposed to win any fight he starts."

I tried to guess what she meant by that, what was hidden in her words. She smiled at me, and, Lord, what a smile that was. Her lips were as dark red as berries, her teeth white and even. Her eyes could hold a man, and she knew they could. They were big eyes, bright green with sparks to them, like pools in a shady forest. They had heavy lids and thin brows that slanted.

Gentlemen, she could fetch air man who called himself a man. I was put to it to recollect other fair women I'd known. Like Winnie, who'd once called me the man sent from God whose name was John. Vandy Millen, who'd sung me into her unforgotten song. Donie Carawan, who'd repented me her bad sins. Others. But mostly I recollected little Evadare, so fair-haired and lovely, the one I loved best of all. The thought of her was a shining light to me just then.

"Come this way, John," Tiphaine bade me, and she winnowed as she led me through the door into the next room.

"I sense that you're rather an extraordinary man," she said.

I was a-looking round that room, and it was sure enough a big, square one, and it was purely rich. All round the walls it was hung with curtains of dark cloth, velvet as I reckoned it to be, redder than red wine, red as Tiphaine's red lips. Worked into that cloth were strings of signs, maybe letters in some language I couldn't read. There was a long table with a black, shiny top of polished stuff, and heavy wooden chairs drawn up all round it. From the midmost of the dark, carved beams on the ceiling hung down a ring of pale-shining oil lamps, that gave off a perfumy smell.

"How did you come here to Wolver?" Tiphaine inquired me.

"Why," I said, "I just walked in. From out yonder on the highway, and along the road," and I pointed to the direction I'd come.

"You came along there?" she half-stammered, and for just a second her face went blank. "Past those fires?"

"At the trash dump? Why, sure I did."

"We never use that road when we go to the county seat," she said. "We go by one along the river; or do you know that?"

I nair allowed I knew or didn't know.

"But you did come past the fires, came to us without mishap. You're an extraordinary man, John."

"I do thank you," I decided to say.

"Extraordinary," she repeated. "Here, sit down."

I sat on one of the chairs at the big shiny table, and she took one a-facing me across it.

"I've nair claimed to be a great much," I said. "Just a natural man, but I mostly try to take care of my end when there's aught of trouble."

"Trouble," she said after me. "Look there, you hurt your hand in that fight."

And, God almighty, she was a lovely thing to see as she took my big right hand in both her slim, pale ones with rings on them and pointy, pink nails on the finger ends. She lifted my hand and looked at where I'd cut my knuckles open on Orcutt's hard jaw.

"It's naught to fuss about, ma'am," I said, and I had it in mind that all round me the air in the room had a creepy feel to it.

"Let me cure it for you."

She bent her shining head down. For a second I wondered if she was a-going to kiss my hand. But she only blew on it, with a warm breath, and then she said something. Best I could make out, it sounded like *eerum eirum orrum eurrum neurrum*. And she let go my hand once more, and, you know what? It was all well again, it didn't throb or tingle. It was like as if I'd nair shoved it up against a man's face.

"Better now?" she asked, a-looking up at me.

"All better," I said. "I do thank you."

By then, I had a feeling that I'd do well to get out of there, but she smiled and kept me with her.

"Possibly you'd do well in Wolver, John," she said, a-smiling that smile of hers, and I could see how straight her nose was, how the brows over her eyes were as narrow and smooth as lines drawn by a pen. And she talked like somebody who purely wanted me to stay there.

"What would I do here, Miss Tiphaine?" I inquired her. "I see just some pretty good farm land round about, and what looks to be a mill."

"Call me just Tiphaine," she said, a-giving it to me like an order.

"Tiphaine," I said, and again her smile.

"I would think, John, that we'd decide on what you'd do here," she told me. "It would profit you and us, too. Now, as to a place for you to stay—"

"I don't guess I'll stay just now," I quick decided to put in.

"Not just now, but you'll come back." She wasn't a-making that a question. She told me.

"All right, I'll come back," I said. "Later."

I picked up my guitar and my other stuff. "I'll be a-getting on," I said.

"And you'll come back," she told me again.

"Yessum."

I felt her eyes in my back, all the way out of the room and along the front hall and out through the door.

I walked the path and from the gate I saw the folks at the store, and they all watched me as I started back up the street, on the way I'd come.

I passed the strange yards and strange houses, all of them as quiet as in a picture. I headed my way alongside the sad old ruined church. Beyond that, I looked into the woods, looked again and again. Finally, when I reckoned I was well out of air sight of people in town, I picked a place to walk in amongst dark trees.

The bottom of the blurry sun had touched the mountain tops off yonder, it was a-fixing to set. I'd better make me my camp while I still had light to see by. I struck off a little way through the woods, to where ahead of me I could hear the

singing run of water. That led me to a sort of clump of yew
trees, at the side of a fast, clear-running stream. I dipped
water in my hand to drink, and more to wash my hot face
and neck and ears, then I studied those yews.

They weren't awfully big—maybe the tallest of them was a
tad more than my height—and they had those tight-growing
little needles, and they were yews all right, something you
don't much see in that part of the country. It might could
have been, somebody had planted them there from some
other place. I had it in mind that yew trees are reckoned to
have a good power in them. In England, as I'd heard tell,
they were planted in the burying grounds to keep evil spirits
away. The old-timey English archers had sworn by their bows
of yew, with which they'd whupped and driven the biggest ar-
mies of other nations. So I flung my stuff down amongst
them, where the ground was smooth and would be good to
lie on.

First off I made me a fire, not big but with chunks of hard
wood that would make coals and last a good spell. At the
stream I filled both my old army canteen and the big canteen
cup and fetched them back to the fire, likewise a flat rock
washed clean in the current. Then, before I did aught else, I
picked up the fallen branch of a yew—it was as tough and
springy as wire, would have made a good little bow—and used
it to draw a big circle on the earth round the fire and my
gear. Outside that, I made another, bigger circle, and in the
space betwixt the runs of those two circles I scratched the
twelve signs of the zodiac, the way they'd been taught me by
a fellow named Jackson Warren when he explained me about
lines of protection. Finally I got another yew twig and a piece
of stringy grass and tied the twig across the branch to make a
cross. I hung that to one of the trees overhead.

By that time, the sun had slid down the mountains where
they showed through the trees. A-looking in the dim light
toward where the road was, I could just make out that poor

ruined old church house, and it made me feel bad to look at it. I stirred water and cornmeal together to make a batter and spread it out on my flat rock, to be set close to the fire to bake into a pone. Then I poured coffee and water into a little old pot I had, and propped that on some pebbles so it could boil. I opened one can of sardines for supper.

When my cooking was done, I drank the canteen cup nearly full of hot black coffee and I ate half the pone of cornbread. I hadn't any butter, so I cut off little shavings of cheese to go along with the pone. They tasted right good together. The sardines I ate to the last crumb of them, and I felt better as I dug me a little hole to bury the empty can and the coffee grounds. It was plumb dark by now. The moon, half of it, had come up behind the busted-down old church steeple. The other way off from there, the way I'd walked when I came into Wolver, showed pink light that must come from those fires on the big stretch of the trash dump. They must be a-burning red and murky. I thought of the fires of hell, the way old preachers talk about them to scare the listening sinners.

Round about me in the trees beyond the yew clump, I heard whispery sounds. It was like folks a-telling secrets to one another. And here and there, winky sparks of light. I allowed they must be reflections of my little campfire on leaves, but they had the look of eyes. Watching eyes.

Over in my mind I turned over a sight of things that had happened, the standoffish way of the folks in the Wolver yards, the fight with Ottom Orcutt and how he'd been surprised at how it turned out, matters like that; but mostly about the woman called Tiphaine, all her drowning beauty and all her way of a queen on this earth, or at least the earth where Wolver was. And the things she'd said to me, and the things she'd likewise left unsaid. And what those things might could possibly mean.

Part of what they possibly meant grew in my mind. I took

my guitar and tuned it. Then I picked, and in a soft mutter I
sang an old song to myself:

> Lady, I never loved witchcraft,
> Never dealt in privy wile,
> But evermore held the high way
> Of love and honor, free from guile.

A-singing that was a sort of help. Not so much whisper
now in the woods round about me, and the flickers of light
that looked like eyes didn't flicker so much.

At last I got to the feeling that I was tired. I'd come a long
chunk of a way that day, had done a sight of walking, had
fought fist and skull with a strong man. I yawned, and it did
me good to yawn. So I spread out my two blankets next the
fire and laid aside my hat and dragged off my old boots and
stretched out to sleep. It was a-coming on to be a little bit
chilly, so I rolled up in the blanket and lay close to the
warmth of the fire.

The half moon had climbed up, and its light was dim instead of clear. I looked up at it. There should ought to be a
spangle of stars round it, but I could barely make them out,
couldn't see the constellations I knew. They made what
looked like strange, faint patterns, though maybe that was
because my eyes had got themselves tired and blurry.

Almost right away I went to sleep, as sound as I'd ever
been since I was born on this earth.

CHAPTER 3

A mockingbird sang so loud up over me that I waked up in the first gray-colored morning light. No stars looked out as the sun showed its first pink in the misty east. I sat up and looked round me, a-thinking about breakfast.

Half my pone of bread was left over from supper. I stirred what was left of my coals of fire and put new wood on them. Then I filled up the coffeepot and set it near enough to heat, and I propped my flat stone where it would warm itself, too. Then I took my razor and a sliver of soap and a little mirror out of my soogin sack and walked barefoot to the stream.

My hand told me the water was cold, but I shucked off my shirt and jeans pants and flung myself down in it to wash all over. That was sure enough a tingly good feeling. A-coming out again, I got my clothes back on and soaped my face and made out to shave. By the time I got back to my fireside, there was light enough to see all round the circles I had drawn for my camp.

Here and yonder, amongst a scatter of toadstools and bits of tufty moss, I saw tracks.

I bent down for a closer look. They were sort of paw-tracks, not plain enough to be sure what sort of thing had made them. I reckoned they went two and two, not four and four, so whatever had been there had been up on two legs to scout on me. But I noted that none of the tracks showed inside my circles, none of them even nearby; which meant that the scouter hadn't felt like crowding close. I was glad to note that thing. A-sitting down, I got on my socks and boots.

By that time the coffee was boiled and I poured me some, and then I put three nice, thick slices of bacon on the hot stone to fry. I sipped coffee till the bacon was crisp, and I ate it with the cold pone and had me more coffee. Finally I cleaned the place up, and while I cleaned I studied about what to do.

What I'd only started to learn about Wolver must be learnt the whole way. In any case, that Tiphaine lady had bidden me to come back, and back was where I meant to come. That was my sworn duty. My duty to Wolver, and to the government that had sent me there.

But first off, I'd better stow my things out of sight and go on in without them. The day before, I'd been sort of pestered awhile because I'd had to look after my guitar. Today, it just purely wouldn't go into Wolver with me. The thing to do was hide it somewhere else than the place I'd made my camp, where whatever it was had come a-nosing round.

So I rolled up the blankets round my guitar and put my coffeepot in the soogin sack and headed into the woods along the stream. I came to some laurels, grown thick and close together as a hedge, a pure down hell of them. I studied them and figured me a way to get in amongst them so nobody else would figure it out, too. I stacked up my stuff betwixt the roots of two big ones and yanked off branches to fling over it and hide it. Then I went out another way, careful as I could, and on back down the stream. All I carried now was my canteen at my belt.

Out on the road again, I saw that sunup had come, and it looked to be no clearer a sky than the day before, with the air sort of close-feeling and warm. I slogged on back past the beat-up church and into Wolver.

Again, folks looked at me from their doors, but didn't speak me air word. I got along to opposite that great big house where Tiphaine lived, and saw the little one across from it where Ottom Orcutt seemed like to have a black-smith forge. I heard a hammer to ring out, and went into the yard. There was an open shed up against the house, and in it burned the forge fire. Ottom Orcutt stood at an anvil, a-pounding with a hammer.

"Well," he said, and grinned his teeth at me in a smutty face. "Here you are again."

"I was asked back, Mr. Orcutt," I said.

"Not so much of the mister round here, John," he said. "Folks just call me Ottom, and let it go at that." He grinned his teeth at me again. "You know, I took it right hard, that there whupping you gave me yesterday in front of the folks. But it might could be we'd get to know one another."

"I do hope you're right," I said to him. "I'd like that. Now, I'm a-going to the store."

"See you round." And those words from him sounded friendly.

I walked on past the shed and up on the porch of the store. Three–four men, they might could have been some of the ones who'd been there the day before, lounged here and there. They looked at me, they nodded. First time I'd had that from air soul I'd met first off in Wolver. I went in, and the storekeeper lady, Eula Jarboe, said, "Yes?" in a nearabout neighborly way.

"I wanted to buy me a couple more things to eat, ma'am," I told her.

I found two nice sweet potatoes in a basket, a can of green beans and another of boiled onions, some crackers, and two cans of fruit, peaches and greengage plums. She put them in a paper poke for me. While I was a-counting money out from my pocket for them, a soft voice said my name, "John."

I looked up. It was that blond girl who'd fooled with my guitar the first day. Lute Baynor, I'd heard them name her. "You ain't got your guitar," she said.

"No," I said back. "I put it away when I came over this morning."

"Tiphaine sent to tell you, come over to the house. Come on, I'll walk you there."

So Tiphaine had sent her to get me, and she'd walk me over to make sure I'd go. "All right, Miss Lute," I said. "I was on my way there."

"Just call me Lute." She smiled, and her smile was a pretty one. "If you call me Miss Lute, that makes me to sound old enough to be your grandmother."

We walked out together and the men on the porch watched us while we crossed the street. I could feel their eyes on the back of my shirt. I reckoned they were pure down curious about me.

We went in through the gate and up the walk betwixt those pale flowers I could recognize, up to the big heavy old door with all its hinges and lock. I put up my fist to knock, but the door opened and there stood Tiphaine in all that drowning beauty she knew she had.

"Good morning, John," she sort of half-sang to me. "Thank you, Lute. You may go now, but remember you're due here at sundown."

"Yes, yes, of course," said Lute, and turned and trotted off away, a-taking the order.

"Come in, John," Tiphaine bade me. She was dressed in a sort of green robe that shone like silk, that had red silk workings at its neck and sleeves and hemline. When she moved, the robe rustled. Round her temples, to tie back her storm of shining black hair, was a red band set with green jewels. "Come in," she said again, and held the door wide for me.

I came into the hallway and set down my things I'd bought. Then I had me a look at the horned woman-thing statue.

"Very well, John," she halfway chuckled in her throat, "what's your considered judgment of my image?"

"Why," I said, "I'm no great much educated in art, but I'd reckon to say it's startling."

She did laugh then. "A sound critical opinion. That's the Earth Mother, John, and not even I can tell you how many thousands of years ago it was carved out. But just now, I'm having some breakfast, and I hope you'll join me."

She led me past her statue to that same inner door I remembered and took me into the inner room she had, all hung round about with the red velvet and its strings of letters I couldn't for the life of me read. On the bright tabletop was spread a white cloth, and on the cloth were set dishes. "Sit down," she said, the same way she'd said it the day before, and took the place opposite me.

"I've already had a bait of my own for breakfast," I said.

"Well, at least have coffee with me."

She took up a brown china pot and poured from it into a white mug. "Cream and sugar?" she inquired me.

"No, I do thank you, I like it black."

I waited till she'd filled another mug, then I reached out and took that one. "I've heard old-timey folks say that there's luck in a changed cup," I allowed.

She smiled her utter sweetest. "You're truly a prudent man, John," she said. "Did you suspect that I meant to poison you? But I wouldn't do that, not for money." She took up the cup I'd left her and sipped. "Because," she said, "I feel, I am sure, that you could be highly useful and happy here in Wolver."

I drank some coffee, too. It was strong and good. "I thank you, Tiphaine," I said to her, "but useful and happy in what respect?"

"Oh come, you're perceptive enough to realize that by now you've made something of a sensation in this quiet little village of ours," she told me, a-smiling. "I don't mean just by walking in as a stranger and immediately having your own way—"

"My own way?" I repeated her. "Hold on now, I nair yet much studied over a-having my own way. And sure enough, not here in Wolver."

She sat and ate some of a little white cake, with bits of dried fruit in it. She held out the plate to me, but again I said, "No, I thank you, I've had me some breakfast."

"And you're still being prudent. Circumspect."

I was, a trifle bit, but I smiled and shook my head. "I'm just sort of a-wondering," I told her. "A-wondering what you think it is you want of me."

"To give you valuable help, perhaps. Where did you spend last night, John?"

"Why, off someplace in the woods." I wasn't about to tell her just exactly where. "That's an old story with me. I'm used to a-making camp different places in my wanderings."

She put down her coffee cup, and the jewels shone on her finger rings. "Why don't you stop your wanderings, right here in Wolver? It would most certainly profit you."

"Wolver," I repeated after her. "How's Wolver run? What sort of place is it?"

Tiphaine told me.

Wolver had been a mill town once, years back, and then the mill had closed down and the road rebuilt to run off, miles away from Wolver. But folks lived in the old houses and kept things a-running, betwixt themselves. Children went to the public schools at the county seat, just to keep the law from a-bothering round. But mostly Wolver folks kept to themselves, because, Tiphaine said, Wolver was that kind of place. No electricity—not even at the mill, it was run by steam. No telephones. No running water.

"How do the folks live here?" I inquired her. "How do they make money to live on?"

"They make a lot of the things they need without money coming into it. They remember old wisdoms, old skills. Most

of them farm in some way, big or little. We grind our own
meal and flour. The textile mill's been opened again, to make
clothing labels for a big firm up north—about twenty or
twenty-five people work there and draw wages. Mr. Quill
Norbury acts as manager. And sometimes we ship out homemade products at a profit. The women weave fine fabrics.
There's some pottery—interesting pottery. This coffeepot and
these mugs were made here. Then Ottom Orcutt is a skillful
smith. His hand-wrought ironwork fetches a ready price for
us."

For us, she'd said, not for Ottom Orcutt. It sounded like a
community business.

"Ottom Orcutt," I said the name after her. "I was a-talking to him just a few minutes back. He doesn't seem to hold
that fight against me."

"No, he doesn't," she said in her singing voice. "More than
anything else, I judge that he's mystified about you. You see,
Ottom's not supposed to lose his fights."

I kept myself from a-staring. "You mean, he's got him
some system of self-defense?"

"I agree that you might call it something of that sort, John.
But the point is, it didn't seem to work with you at all, which
could mystify others beside Ottom." All the time, she had
those bright, shining eyes of hers on me. "It could be that
you're destined to stay here among us, to develop yourself, so
to speak, in Wolver."

She narrowed her eyes, like as if to make a study on me.
"You know," she said, "you could be described as imposing."

"Imposing?" I repeated her. "No, ma'am, I nair tried to
impose on folks, no way at all."

"That's not what I meant at all, though possibly you're
just having fun with a play on words." Still she made her
study. "I mean, you have a definite presence. You're as tall as
any man in Wolver—taller. You carry those wide shoulders

and that straight back quite well, John. And your face, you have a fine, straight nose and a strong set to the jaw. And your long dark hair becomes you, though it's not as dark as mine."

"Nor yet air sight as pretty," I said.

She laughed. "There now, and you're a charmer of sorts in your conversation. Nor do I think this is all facade, either. I sense a good mind, a strong personality, and a certain exercise of most interesting gifts."

"Well," I said, "I do thank you kindly."

Her eyes hung to mine. "If you stay, you would be bound to develop into a leader, an important figure, here in Wolver. You may think that we're only a small community and in some ways an odd one, but I can promise you that the opportunities here are considerable."

"What way could I be a leader?"

"For that, you'd have to be made ready by instruction." She half-sang the words at me again. "Leadership here goes hand in hand with scholarship, John. You'd have to be taught from our Book of Life yonder."

She waved her hand over to a side table in a corner, where there lay a big book with black, shaggy covers. I reckoned it must be bound in the hide of one of those cattle they call Black Angus.

"When you read in that," she said, "it will profit you greatly. Its wisdom is as precious as jewels. Speaking of jewels, do you like them, John? What do you think of this pearl on my forefinger?"

She laid her slim, soft hand on the table. The ring, as I made a guess, was gold, and it had a stone maybe the size of a robin's egg, a sort of soft sheeny white. In it crawled a rosy light that shone through, moved, winked.

"Well now," I said, a-studying it, "that's a right pretty thing, for a fact. Must be it's worth a right much of money."

"It's priceless," she said softly. "It's beyond value. The man who dived deep, deep in the ocean to bring it back gave it to me because he felt he must. Now," and her voice went to a soft drone, "look at it, John. Look at it."

I looked. The pearl seemed to glow brighter. That rosiness inside it made another stirring, flowing move.

"Look at it," Tiphaine bade me again in her tuneful soft voice. And, gentlemen, I looked.

That pearl thing blurred, like as if there was some kind of steam round about it. My ears set up a tired hum. My eyelids took themselves on a heavy feeling. Maybe if I closed them they'd stay closed, so I didn't close them. I felt that if I shook my head it would clear up, but the shake of it would show Tiphaine that I wasn't about to drop over asleep. There was a close feeling round about me now, like as if somebody was a-wrapping my head up in cloth. I mustn't go under, that much I knew.

In my half-dreamy mind I groped out the lines of a song I'd been taught long years back by a wise old man named Uncle T. P. Hinnard, and silently in my heart I said them over:

> *Three holy kings, four holy saints,*
> *At heaven's high gate that stand,*
> *Speak out to bid all evil wait*
> *And stir no foot or hand . . .*

It worked for me. My head cleared, the hum died down in my ears. I told myself that no man yet had disgraced himself by a-saying such words.

The hum tried to start back, and I fought against it. This time, I said to myself, "Though I walk in the valley of the shadow of death, I shall fear no evil." I mustn't fear it. Face it but mustn't fear it.

"Now you begin to feel tired, John," Tiphaine was a-saying

to me, slow and soft and tuneful, and the pearl on her finger shone like a rosy star. "You've wandered so far. Poor, tired John."

How gentle her voice was. How musical.

"You're so tired, so tired with all your wanderings. Here, here is where you can find rest and happiness and strength for yourself. Here among us in Wolver. You can be so happy here. You can be great."

I sat where I was and harked at her with my eyes only half closed up. I decided to give my head a little nod at her. No more than that.

"You will listen to the voices I summon for you, John," she told me, and she sounded as sure about it as if it had happened already. "Voices of great wisdom and great strength. I will tell you wonderful names, John. Let them take strong hold of your heart and your memory."

I made her another nod with my head, made it look drowsy. But the blur was gone off from my eyes, the hum was out of my ears. I looked at that shining pearl on her ring, and I felt sure of myself. Whatever hand Tiphaine was a-playing with me, I had a hand of my own to play against her.

"Now listen to the names I will speak, John. Belphegor. Tetragrammaton. Lucifer."

Those were names I'd heard before that, the last one specially. Lucifer . . . Now, all of a sudden quick, the whole thing fell into place for me. Now I knew right well what it was in Wolver the government had sent me to seek out the truth of.

"How art thou fallen from heaven, O Lucifer, son of the morning," Tiphaine spaced the words out like a prayer. "Our father, who wert in heaven, how thou shalt rise again to heaven, and that soon, brighter than ever before."

That flat told me that my guess was right about what went on in Wolver.

Silence then, a couple–three moments. I could hear Tiphaine as she breathed deeply, in and out. I heard my own self a-breathing. Inside myself I said me another strong prayer, to help keep my mind clear.

"John," she said to me, in a stronger voice, "now you are ready to do what I command you."

I nair replied her one mumbling word. I only looked at her under my half-shut eyelids. I saw her get up, with a whisper of her green robe.

"Stand up on your feet, John," she ordered me. "Come along here, beside me."

Slow as slow, I rose from the chair and stood with my feet wide apart, my eyelids still kept at their droop. Out came her long hand and took tight hold of mine.

"Come," she said again, clear and commanding.

I walked with her, a-making my steps slow and heavy. We went side by side to the door of the room, and out into that front hall. She led me along to where the black statue stood all ugly and crouched down, and there she made me stop.

"The Earth Mother, John," said Tiphaine. "The very oldest of all worshipped things. There were goddesses for humanity to worship before there were gods. Speak her name, John."

"Earth Mother," I sort of mumbled.

"Worship her now. Kneel before her."

I just stood, straddle-legged, with my head sort of limped over.

"Kneel, I say." Her voice had gone sharp, almost angry. "Kneel down and kiss her feet."

That was when I straightened myself up and opened my eyes wide. All across my face I spread the biggest grin I could make.

"No, Tiphaine," I said. "I don't reckon I'll do that thing."

CHAPTER 4

The two of us stood there together, face to face, by that black stone thing that was both woman and animal and named Earth Mother. Tiphaine downright goggled at me. I could see the whites of her eyes, all the way round the green. I could tell that, just for the once in her life, she'd plumb forgotten how man-killing beautiful she was. That rich, red mouth of hers had gone pale. It wiggled itself like a worm on a hook before she could make it say air word to me.

"Who are you?" she half squeaked. "What are you?"

"You already know that. They call me John. I've been a-trying to deserve that good name my whole life long."

"No, no, I mean who sent you here to Wolver?"

Naturally I wasn't about to tell her the government had sent me, so I nair replied her one word. I simply kept quiet and grinned her again.

"You didn't kneel down when I told you," she said, like as if it pestered her to death. "You weren't even touched by my spell, not even touched. You looked at my pearl, but—"

She didn't finish it, she just goggled again.

"That pearl's a right pretty thing," I said. "It must be worth quite some money. But no, ma'am, it didn't put a spell on me, none whatever."

"Then you—" Again she broke off and looked at me. "Did they tell you to come here and depose me? Take my place?"

I laughed, as much to make myself easy as aught else. "No, Tiphaine, nothing like that. I just came on through here, a-going to and fro in the world, and a-walking up and down in it."

I wondered myself if she knew who first said that thing, at the start of the book of Job. If she did know, she nair said she did. She'd gone into a whole other line of thought. Her face had turned as pale as white wool, with her eyes and her mouth gone hard in it.

"Possibly you think you're having fun with me, here in my own house," she said, betwixt her white teeth. "What if I was to call out just a single word? And my friends would come into this hall and kill you and throw you into a hole out of sight, what then?"

"I reckon I can answer that one," I told her right back. "I wouldn't lie long in that hole before some fellows I know would show up in Wolver, to see if they couldn't fetch me back into sight again. And they'd ask a good few impudent questions to find out how come I'd been killed."

That fetched her. She shrunk herself back away from me then. Her head bobbed and her black hair stirred on it. Her bosom went up and down and up and down, like a pump handle in a windstorm. Because, gentlemen, I'd scared her. And that was something I don't reckon happened to her many days of her life.

She tried to give me a smile then, and it was a trembly one.

"What you say makes me know that my first guess was right, John," she said, music in her voice again. "You come here from—from those who are higher than I am. I'm afraid that that means they mistrust me."

"Why should they mistrust you?" I inquired her.

She didn't rightly answer that one. "You must be here to see if I'm doing what I'm ordered to do, what it's my duty to do. John, why am I being mistrusted?"

"If I knew," I said, "would I be supposed to tell you?"

"At least you tell me you haven't come to Wolver to take my place away from me."

"No," I decided to say. "Not that exactly."

"Come back in here." She moved toward the curtained

room where she'd tried to put her spell on me with her pearl ring. "Come in and sit down again, and talk to me." Once again, her trembly smile. "I have some special wine, such wine as you don't often have a chance to taste. You and I can drink together, to a better acquaintance. Please. I'm sorry I tried to—to do what I thought I could do to you."

By then she'd got hold of herself again. She was a-trying to turn her beauty back on me.

"Can't you forget that I tried to threaten you?" she almost begged to me. "Come and sit down with me and let's talk."

"I do thank you, but not right away now. I've got to go somewhere."

"And you don't dare say where that is." That was a dare on her own part, for me to speak up and say it.

I grinned her as before. "Most times I don't take dares, Tiphaine. But the point is, you don't dare ask me where."

"No," she agreed me. "No, I don't. I shouldn't have said what I just said."

"Let's just have it that I'd better go follow the orders I've been given," I suggested to her.

She sighed and then she smiled, and well I knew that it was still a tad of trouble for her to smile.

"Tonight, this very night," she said, "as though you don't already know. When midnight is past, there comes a special night, John. Some of us will be in this house at sundown, to prepare for it. Wouldn't you be nice enough to come and join us?"

"Sure enough, Tiphaine," I granted her. "I'll be right glad to do that thing. But just now, I'll be a-going."

"No hard feelings, John?" she pleaded.

"None whatever," I said, for right then I didn't have aught of hard feelings toward her. "Good-bye till sundown, Tiphaine."

I took up my poke of rations and went to the door. She

stood right where she was by the statue. I could feel her a-watching my back. A-watching me with those scared green eyes.

Outside, as I came out through the gate in the hedge, I saw Ottom Orcutt in front of his forge, and with him was the tallow-pudgy fellow who'd first talked fight with me on the porch of Eula Jarboe's store house. Ottom flung up his hand to me, and walked over thattaway.

"You and Tiphaine been a-having some talk?" he inquired me.

"We did swap a waif word or two," I told him.

"What was it youins talked about?" asked tallow-pudgy.

I gave him a look all the way up and down. "I nair was such a gone gump as to talk private business outside," I said. "Anyway, I'll be back here come sundown."

"Sundown," Eula Jarboe repeated me from her store porch where she'd been a-harking at us. "You'll be back come sundown?"

"You've sort of come to town here, John," allowed Ottom.

"We'll be a-seeing you sundown, then," Eula Jarboe called over.

"I reckon," I said, and walked off. They watched me go, the same way Tiphaine had watched me, though maybe not quite so scary-eyed.

Yet again I tramped along the street, past those strange-looking houses where pinch-faced little children watched from the yards and sneaky-eyed grown-up folks watched from the doors and windows. But not a one of them made to follow after me. Where did they reckon I would take myself? Or did they even dare reckon about that? I was purely a mystery to them, they were out of the notion of a-crowding me or a-seeing where I might go ransacking off to beyond Wolver. Whither I went, thither I came, as the old saying says. And they didn't make it their business to find out, not so far at least.

I got out of Wolver. Far behind, I felt they watched me

and wondered. I made my way past the pitiful, ruined-down church house, and past that to where I'd stayed all night in the woods. One more time I took me a long look in all directions, to make sure again that no soul would be on watch, and I saw nobody. Then I slid in amongst the trees.

I came to the place under the yews where I'd camped out the night before. Naught showed that it had been bothered with at all. There I set down the rations I'd bought. I meant to eat supper before I went here and there to pick up chunks of hard firewood. With my knife I shaved up some dead pine twigs for lighter, and made a little, close-packed cooking fire that wouldn't send up smoke to show where I was. When it had caught on to stay, I went to the laurel thicket where I'd hidden my gear. Nothing had been there either, I made sure. I sat down on a twisty sycamore root by the stream, to pick guitar softly and do me a spell of thinking.

So far, so good, you might could say; but you could likewise say, so good only so far, and there was far yet to go. I'd come along to where I was on such thin ice I could near about hear it crackle under my feet.

I'd played the bluff game with Tiphaine, a thing I don't much care to do, and I'd won it, anyway the first hand of it. She'd talked mean about a-having me killed and flung in a lonely hole, but I'd come up with the right reply for that and I'd walked off from her with her scared eyes. So far so good, I said it to myself again. But I thought over that talk of hers about a-having me killed and hidden away. On my guitar I softly picked a song it brought to mind:

> 'There's many a man been killed on a dark night
> And cast in a lonely grave . . .

If that happened to me, I'd not have to worry about the ones who'd come after me to carry my bones away.

By now, though, I was sure of what up to then I'd only guessed about the Wolver crowd.

Witchcraft. A worn-out word, one that made you think of

Hallowe'en parties for little baby children. There was another, better word. Devil-worship. What the scholars call diabolism.

I'd been a-knowing about witches all my born days. I mean the pure quill, the sure-enough fact of the thing, not this stuff that kids have lately been a-getting out of books about covens and Sabbats, those little squibs of stuff they read to make them think they know it all. It's like a-dipping into something about Karl Marx or Zen Buddhism, and a-thinking you know that. No, gentlemen, I've been up against the genuine old-timey article of witchcraft in this life of mine.

No way had all of them I've known been women, such as most folks think of when they think about witches at all. He-witches I've heard called warlocks, a creepy-sounding word for creepy-sounding goings on. I recollected Mr. Onselm and his Ugly Bird that shared his life with him so close that if you killed the one, you killed the other; Mr. Howsen, blind in one eye, who'd served the thing called One Other in the Bottomless Pool way up on top of Hark Mountain; Mr. Loden, who nair quite got to live out the three hundred years he'd been promised by let's not mention who; Shull Cobart, who'd traded with that selfsame party for a black fiddle that could play down air fiddler in the wide world; Forney Meechum, who'd wound up as a ghost corked into a bottle in a hollow tree.

Women witches, too. One of them I figured I'd been just as lucky not to meet face to face—Polly Wilse, a-sitting all those long lifetimes in her desrick on Yandro, with strange things a-using round to do her bidding. Almost without a thought to it, I picked me another song, soft as a whisper:

In the pines, in the pines, where the sun never shines,
I shiver when the wind blows cold . . .

Not that it blew cold right then and there by the creek, but I did shiver myself, or anyway I hiked up my shoulders.

Those witches and warlocks I'd come up against had had ugly powers to do ugly things, bought at I couldn't rightly swear what price, though I had my suspicions. They could cause sickness and whirlwinds and seven years of bad luck, they could make the rain pour forth and the rivers boil, they could do all kinds of trouble. But mostly where I'd run into them would be just the one witch-man or witch-woman, alone and mean as hell, amongst families of more or less decent folks, folks they could scare or fool into a-paying them for what they did or a-paying them to keep them from a-doing it.

But that wasn't the way of things yonder in Wolver. By now, I could pretty well figure that the whole settlement wasn't only run by the witch belief, there had to be witchcraft and its fear and service in each house and each yard, in each thing each man, woman or child did all day and all night long. It was just a little town of devil worshippers.

And all that was a-going on went on right there in Wolver. Take Ottom Orcutt. From what Tiphaine had hinted to me, he had some charm or other that was to make him to win all his fights. I'd seen such charms, in the *Albertus Magnus* book, what's called the *Grand Albert*, and in *The Long Lost Friend*, though I myself haven't air used them in my own fights. When I was up against Ottom, I just fought him. I'd beat him to the punch a couple–three times, then I'd clustered my own punches till down he went. And he'd been more surprised over it than mad with me. He hadn't figured on that to happen with me, to happen with air man he fought skull and knuckle in Wolver.

But if Ottom had that charm to beat whatair man he fought—though somehow it hadn't worked with me—why did he just stay in Wolver and hammer out iron things at his forge? Why not go out into the world and fight a champion and win a title, with all the money and glory? The answer to that had to be, he must stay where he was. It might could be that his charm was good only in Wolver, till I happened through.

That, or either Tiphaine wouldn't let him go, she made him to stay. Something or other of that sort.

While I touched my silver guitar strings, I ran through the whole thing in my mind. I thought over how the general run of folks believes witches work. Another song came to my memory, one that had scared me a right much when I was just a chap:

The woods are full of goblins and most of them are bad,
They chase the witches flying through the air,
And should an old witch catch you while riding on her
    broom,
Your folks would never find you anywhere . . .

Likely there was some grain of truth in the song. As for the men-witches, the ones called warlocks, there seemed like to be those, too, in Wolver. Bird-faced little Quill Norbury, the boss man at the mill, who'd started out with me by a-trying to give me orders. And Ottom Orcutt, the smith—he was supposed to have his special ways to win fights, though the ways hadn't come true when he'd messed with me. These men fitted into the organization, it was plain enough.

For witches have organization, and right yonder at Wolver, just along the road I was coming to know right well, they were plumb all broken out with it. In my time I'd read and likewise heard about such a thing. I'd made it my business to find out in my work, the work I'd wound up being sent to Wolver for. Witches made up into what they called covens, most usually twelve of them with a thirteenth one for a sort of chief. It wasn't always exactly thirteen in a coven—up in Connecticut long years ago, there'd been a coven of twelve at Hartford, another of eleven at Stratford—but the number didn't seem to vary much. Thirteen in a coven; might could that be why thirteen is reckoned to be an unlucky number?

I got up and headed back to where I'd built my fire. The sun was a-moving westward in that dull sky, and when it went down I'd be due at Tiphaine's house in Wolver. I saw that the wood had burnt down the way I'd meant it to, into coals amongst ashes. I shoved my two sweet potatoes deep in, with coals and ashes over them, to bake. Then I sat down and did me another chunk of thinking.

It was a sure enough fact that Tiphaine must rule the settlement, but it went farther than that, farther than just what seemed like to be a-going on in Wolver. Because Tiphaine figured that I must have come there from some other place, that I'd been sent there to look into what she did, maybe push her out and take over and rule things instead of her. Which added up to Wolver a-being just one part of a big, big thing that stretched all over this country. It would be like a labor union, like a church, like a great big old secret society. All of that made good sense, when I put my mind to it. But so far, it was just a guess, what school folks call an educated guess. It wasn't really enough for the report I'd been told to fetch back. I still had work to do; and it might could be dangerous work.

I sat beside my fire and looked here and yonder in the woods all round about. You all have done that, I reckon, and know how it works out.

You look and study over clumps and tuds of leaves a-growing on the different trees, and after while they seem like as if they turn into faces, with the dark spots amongst the green tangle to make eyes and mouths. Some of them are like folks' faces, here and there maybe long and beaky for the nose, now and then with leaf-bunches at the side to make ears. With a few of such faces you see bare branches stuck up at the top, always two at a time, like the forky horns of buck deer. Other faces are like animal faces, dogs or bobcats or bulls or lizards. Then, here and there on a big stout tree trunk, knots in the bark squirm together into faces. And you look at them and they look back at you. They can hold your eyes to theirs. None of such things are what you'd call pretty or friendly, but you keep on a-looking at them till it gets hard to pull your look from them.

I studied the leafy faces back and forth and figured to myself, it must have been like that with the very first men on this earth, a-seeing faces pop out amongst the trees where they lived, and a-knowing the trees were as much alive as they were their own selves. It might could be that that's how come the people used to worship trees, the oak and the ash and the others.

But I wasn't a-letting the face-shapes spell me. Tiphaine hadn't managed that, and neither would they. All the while I picked my guitar, soft whispers, little tags and scraps of tunes. Now and then I tried to make up a song for myself. I do that lots of times, with words to go with them. Like:

> I got off the bus on the highway,
> Down the old side road I came,
> Till I made it down to a little small town
> With Wolver for a name.

> What is its light or darkness,
> What is its prayer or curse?
> Does that name mean that wolves are seen,
> Or maybe something worse?

I reckoned I'd have to work that one over some, but it asked the question I'd asked myself.

When I figured the potatoes were done, I raked them out and split them and stuck in bits of cheese. I ate them with crackers and a cup of water. While I ate, I kept on a-studying.

By the time I finished and cleaned up, I could see the dull sun through the treetops yonder to the west. It had worked itself pretty close down to the mountain ridge. By the time it set, I was due to be at Tiphaine's house down yonder in Wolver, for whatever she hoped would be the reason for me to come. And it was up to me to get started right soon.

I washed my face and hands good in the branch, and got out my comb and swept my long hair into some kind of decent order. Then I picked up my guitar and set out on the gravelly road.

CHAPTER 5

When I tramped in along Wolver's gravelly main street this time, the folks at all the houses gave me their long looks from their doors and windows and yards. In front of one place stood some little rough-dressed children, their eyes on me as tight as buttons on a shirt, and round the corner of the house poked out a round, brown head, either another child or some creature I didn't know, a-looking, too. The old folks stood together at the open door, a-gopping at me like the youngins and a-saying something to one another. Likely it was something like, "Yonder comes John, a-headed for Tiphaine's place." I had it in mind, the folks of Wolver had begun to know who I was, had begun to figure on me.

And figure what?

The last rays of the sun had turned from red to rose on the mountain top as I got to Tiphaine's big hedged-in house, in along that bushy-bordered front path and up on the porch. I swung the big brass knocker ring where it hung in the monkey jaws, and right off quick the door opened inward. It was little Quill Norbury there, all dressed up fine in a powder-blue slack suit with saddle-stitched lapels, and he had a bright red scarf tucked in round his skinny neck.

"Oh," he said, his eyes popped out at me. "John. Come right in the house, John, Tiphaine said we could expect you."

In I came as he bade me, past where the Earth Mother statue waited with its curly horns and its look of a woman and beast in one. Norbury walked ahead of me through the hallway into the inside room.

A bunch of folks sat at the table in there. On the table was spread a cloth embroidered in letters I didn't know, like the ones on the hangings at the walls. There were glasses set out and a big crockery wine jug. Overhead glittered the ring of lamps.

At the head of the table, in a black wooden chair with padded arms, sat Tiphaine, in all her beauty she knew so well she had. She was dressed in another close-clinging robe, this time of gleamy black cloth, probably silk again, with a pattern of gold thread worked up and down on it. Others were Ottom Orcutt, the blacksmith, who had on what must have been his best brown suit of store clothes; Eula Jarboe, the storekeeper lady, her hair stuck here and there with shiny jewel things; and the blond girl Lute Baynor, in a nice green frock, with a nervous look in her blue eyes. Norbury took a chair next to Tiphaine. One empty seat was left, the other end of the table from Tiphaine. She pointed to it with the hand that wore the pearl ring.

"You may sit there, John," she said, like as if she was a-making me the lucky winner of a prize. "There, opposite me. I see that you brought your guitar with you. Good."

"Most times I fetch it along where I go," I said, as I sat down with the guitar across my lap.

"Friends," she said, and looked on all the others, all the way round the table. "You who come here tonight to sit with me. I'll ask John to sing whatever song he might think appropriate for a gathering like this."

"Yes," said Quill Norbury, with half a husk in his skinny throat.

"If you truly want me to," I said, for I'd thought of the right song for that place, and I touched the string. "Here's one I just so happened to read one time in a book, and put a tune to it myself."

Their eyes were on me, their shiny eyes. Amongst the cur-

tains on the walls, seemed like there was a stir and a whisper.
I sang:

> I last night lay all alone
> On the ground, and heard the mandrake groan;
> And plucked him up, though he grew full low,
> And as I had done, I heard the cock crow.

They nodded at that and grinned to one another, more
than I thought the song was worth. "Mandrake," said Tiphaine from the other end of the table. "We're acquainted
with the mandrake. Go on, John, another verse, if you
know one."

I sang another verse, one that always sort of chilled me:

> A murderer yonder was hung in chains,
> The sun and the wind had shrunk his veins;
> I bit off a sinew, I clipped his hair,
> I brought off his rags, that danced in the air.

Then I stopped, with my palm flat on the strings to hush
them.

"Go on," said Tiphaine again, like as if she gave me an
order. "Sing the rest of it."

I set the guitar down on the floor. "That's all I know of
the thing," I told her, which wasn't quite the truth. "I got it
from a fellow in Chapel Hill I used to know. He had a book,
Percy's Relics."

"Reliques," said Quill Norbury, the way a teacher sets a
boy right in school. "*Percy's Reliques* is the title."

"And Bishop Percy was quoting from Ben Jonson," added
on Tiphaine. "Rare Ben Jonson, who was no skeptic, who
seemed to know what he put down in what he called *The
Witches' Song.* A good instinct, I suggest, prompted John to
give us those appropriate and tuneful verses."

Her eyes were upon me while she talked, the way ninety-nine men out of a hundred would like to have them, but right that moment I was the hundredth man.

"We liked them immensely," she said, "and we all wish that John could supply others."

"I can supply others," spoke up Quill Norbury, like the teacher's pet.

"Me, too, I think," said Eula Jarboe.

"A little later, perhaps," Tiphaine decided for them. "Or rather, considerably later, after what we must do this night." One more time, she looked round the table at them, and at me. "There is, as all of you are aware, a preparatory ritual for us here. It begins with the partaking of wine, which is the soul of life."

She took up the wine jug. I could see that it had something on it like a picture of spread-out bat wings. All the others passed her up their glasses and she filled them. I sent along my glass last of all, and into it she poured wine as red as the wall curtains, as red as blood, and sent it back to me. She smiled the length of the table at me, the way a specially beautiful fox might could smile outside a chicken run.

"John," she sort of purred, while she filled her own glass, "you reminded me once—earlier today, as a matter of fact—that there's luck in a changed cup. Perhaps you'd like to change cups with me again."

"No, ma'am, I do thank you," I said. "This time I'll just stay with what I've got here."

She laughed at that, like a chime of silver bells.

"How calculating you are, John, and how well you use the sharp wits you were born with. You rationalized at once that if I suggested changing drinks with you, the one I'd already served you was safe."

That was exactly the thing I'd had in mind, but all I said was, "I thank you for that good word about how I think."

"And now," she said, a-giving out with her smile all the

way round, "I'll demonstrate that there was nothing whatever unsafe about the cup I offered to change with John." She lifted her drink high. "My friends, let's all join in a pledge to happiness and triumph in future."

She set her glass to her lovely lips and drank. The others all drank, too. I drank the last of them all, with the feeling that it wouldn't hurt. The wine tasted right good.

"So much for that," said Tiphaine, and put her glass down. "Attention, all. Later tonight, much later, we do that which we are directed to do. But just at present, John is here among us from wherever he came from, he is here to join us. Be one of us. Ottom, bring me the book."

He got up and fetched it from its side table and handed it to her. She flung it open where a funny-looking marker showed midway betwixt its pages. Air soul in that bunch round the table looked hard at her. Me, too, I looked.

"I am your prophetess," said Tiphaine, a-making her voice deep and her words slow. "I am your priestess, for I was ordained your priestess. Hear me, all of you, for I am of the spirit of air, of water, earth, fire."

"Amin," said the others, all of them together. Not amen, amin.

"Hail, you who are here with us," Tiphaine fairly shouted out, and I felt that there was a stir in the hangings on the walls. The fringed bottoms lifted up, like the claws of animals.

"Hail," she said. "You, the air, the sea, the abode! You, the wisdom, the might, the beauty!"

"Amin," all of them said, all of them but me. I started in to tell myself that these things meant what I'd been a-figuring on, a-guessing, from the first minute I'd walked into Wolver.

Tiphaine lifted up her left hand, the one with the ring on it, and signed the cross at them. But she had her thumb up

betwixt her first and second fingers. Once, back when I was
still in the army, an Italian fellow in my outfit had told me
that that was the nastiest, lowest-down way to hold the hand
there ever was.

"So mote it be," the others all droned out. Not might,
mote.

"Hear the words of the Book of Life," said Tiphaine,
a-dropping her hand back to the open page. "Let him whose
name we do not say make the hour auspicious, let him open
to us the gates of life, let him grant us the accomplishment of
true will among us and within us."

Quill Norbury hopped up from where he sat beside her.
He began to move round the table, round it from right to
left, what I've heard called widdershins; the other way from
how the sun goes round, from how the hands of the clock go
on the dial. He stopped a second next to my chair and with
the toe of his foot marked a cross on the floor, close to my
guitar.

"To love me is better than all things," read out Tiphaine,
"for one kiss will you give all. I am all pleasure and purple.
Put on wings and rise before me. Drink to me."

They took up their glasses and drank at her word, all but
Norbury, who was still on his half-dancy way round the table.

"I am the blue-lidded daughter of sunset," said Tiphaine.
"More lovely than you dare to dream."

That sounded more or less like as if she was a-making an
invitation to whoever heard her, but the others only said,
"Amin," said it halfway with a moan in their throats.

Norbury had come back to his chair and sat down, sat
down hard and heavy, like as if that move round the table
had tired him out. Tiphaine read more from her Book of
Life.

"Hail, Earth Mother," she rang out the words, "from
whom all living things are born, to whom all dying things re-

turn. Give unto us the accomplishment of our true wills, our great work. Give unto us the power of life and death over the world that dwells in darkness."

"Amin," they all said the word together.

Another spell of silence. Suddenly I saw, plain as day, what they were up to here in little Wolver.

I'd come smack up against those who looked in the dark places for the power of life and death. I recollected two crazy-headed brothers on Wolter Mountain who called themselves Druids, who tried to raise up old Indian ghost-devils to power them. And the Shonokins at Immer Settlement, who'd claimed to be of a people who'd owned America before the first Indians, and their ugly goings on. Now again, right here, that talk of the power of life and death. Just the same old song by the same old mockingbird; or if it wasn't the same old mockingbird, it might could just as well be—the power of life and death. Who could want that, I wondered myself. Not me, leastways. I didn't want that power over man, woman or child, and I didn't want air living soul to have it over me.

Finally Tiphaine got up. Gentlemen, what a beauty-looking woman she was in her black robe with the gold on it. She commenced her own dancy walk round the table, the opposite direction from Norbury's widdershins move. From left to right she took her way. She stopped for half a second behind my chair and put her hand on my shoulder. I felt like as if her touch burnt through my shirt.

"John," she said, close against my ear. "Meditate in silence, John. The truth will come to you within your heart."

Then she took her hand away. "John," she said, louder, "we rejoice that you have come here. You will join with us, be great and strong among us."

The burning touch of her hand on my shoulder again.

"You'll learn to stand with your head above the heavens, your feet below the hells."

It didn't sound like the thing I wanted to do, not to me it didn't.

She moved a step away. "We do not ask for pacts or bargains," she said, a-looking down at me. "We are not tradespeople, John; you must know that already. There is a giving here, not a trading. There is a great recompense, not a price."

And how important all that sounded, I thought as her hand burnt on my shoulder. All the curtains on the walls stirred and seemed to whisper, near about like half-heard words.

She took up her hand from me at last and went a-shimmering back to her chair and sat herself in it.

"John has been miraculously sent to us," she said to the others. "He came here a perilous way, past the deadly fires. Perhaps he did not fully know the strength that we see in him. But we are glad that he has come here. The time is at hand for us to receive him into our fellowship."

Her eyes looked down at me, lovely, lovely, and how she smiled with her full lips.

"John," she whispered, sweet as honey, "under just what mysterious circumstances, what great auspices, you appear among us, it is perhaps not yet time to decide. You are full of mystery, John, and so are we, here in Wolver."

I didn't speak nor yet move. I waited for what that would lead up to.

"Witchcraft has been misunderstood," she said. "Persecuted. For a while it has been denied. But it has come to be much talked of today, though not often intelligently. Many who profess witchcraft do so with only weak understanding. It needs that they be instructed, educated. If covens everywhere could attain to knowing something, doing something, could unite—very well. We could command governments—not overthrow governments, that is not our direction. We have other directions."

"The thorn in the foot," droned out Eula Jarboe, in a half-sleepy voice. "The fly in the amber."

"Do what thou wilt shall be the whole of the law," said Norbury.

"So spoke Aleister Crowley," nodded Tiphaine. "Great Aleister. Our will is here expressed, and will remain. The word 'witch' means wisdom, and why should wisdom be forbidden? It is a word for enlightenment, progress. Magic began all the sciences. Medicine had its start in Stone Age times, in the hands of wizards. Mystic observers of the skies, the ancient astrologers, begat astronomy. The brilliant experimental mixtures of alchemy gave the world chemistry and physics. Once all these sciences were suspected and condemned and cruelly punished by the established governments and religions."

She waited to let that much sink in. Then:

"The night gods of sorcery, the oldest gods of all, yet seek to benefit and enlighten the whole of mankind. Sorcery is to be honored—revered, followed. Its enemies are to be convicted." Her hands clenched into fists. "Eliminated."

"Amin," they all said, like as if to a prayer. All but me.

"John does not fear the fires of destruction," Tiphaine went ahead, her eyes fastened on me. "He walks past them without fear."

"Without fear," Eula Jarboe repeated her.

"John can return to those fires," said Tiphaine. "He can quench them, set us free from their terror."

"Set us free from their terror," said Eula Jarboe in a hushed-down voice.

"John can be of health and help to us," said Tiphaine, still a-watching me. "Health and help, John. Hear now what I say."

She rolled out what she said, like as if it was in the book before her. Perhaps, somewhere, that's where it was.

"The night gods are here with us, they listen to us, they join us," she said. "They endow us with the wit and will to control nature beyond the natural. Those who doubt, who scoff, their time grows shorter with every moment."

"Amin," went up all the way round the table.

"And you, John," she told me, "when you put out those fires, you will be made foremost among us."

"So mote it be," the others said. One of them, I reckoned, gulped over the words. Quill Norbury? Lute Baynor? I couldn't say for dead certain, but somebody at the table didn't much like what Tiphaine seemed to offer me about being foremost.

And me, I didn't like it air bit.

For, plain as print, Tiphaine wanted me to be in the devilish scheme she talked about, read about. Witchcraft or sorcery, call it how you like, that was what was up, carload lots of it. She had me there amongst them because somehow she reckoned I could do them good in their badness. She reckoned that all she had to do was tell me, "Come," and I'd come. And that wasn't for me.

Her eyes were close on me, lovely again, like as if she and I were there all alone together.

"John," she petted my name with her voice, "you have heard, you understand. You came to Wolver for something, and now you know what it is. We're gathered here to welcome you. How do you present yourself to our fellowship?"

I thought a second, just one second. "Why, as to that," I replied her, "what if I picked and sang you all something?"

"Why, of course, if that's how you will make your answer." She smiled at me. "Sing again."

"Sing again, John," they all of them said after her.

"Sure enough."

Up with my guitar across my knee. I sought me out a couple of chords.

"I'll just do this one," I said. "It so happens that it's likewise in that *Percy's Relics* book we've been a-talking about."

All of them sat and looked and listened. I struck across the silver strings, and I sang:

> In ancient days, tradition shows
> A base and wicked elf arose,
> The Witch of Wokey hight;
> Oft have I heard the fearful tale
> From Sue, and Roger of the vale,
> On some long winter's night.

"Hold on, what's that you're a-giving us?" said one of them, most likely it was Ottom Orcutt, but I paid no mind. I went right ahead with the song:

> From Glaston came a learned wight,
> Full bent to mar her fell despight,
> And well he did, I ween;
> Such mischief nair had yet been known,
> And, since his mickle learning shown,
> Such mischief nair hath been.

"Stop that, this instant!" Tiphaine screamed, shrill as a whistle. "Why are you singing that song against us?"

She had jumped to her feet. The others were up, too, and so was I.

"You meant it for a mockery," Tiphaine accused me.

"Yessum," I kept my voice quiet to say.

"You've deceived us," Tiphaine stammered out at me. "You aren't one of us."

"Recollect that I nair said I was," I told her. "Not one time, remember."

I put my guitar under my arm and headed for the door.

"Wait a second," Ottom Orcutt sort of growled, and started in to follow me. I turned back and stood and looked him all up and down.

"You'd do yourself a favor to leave me be, Ottom," I gave him warning. "You and I had us a little fist and skull yesterday evening, and, the way I recollect it, you didn't have aught the better of it."

He stopped where he was and trembled his cut mouth. "That was outside at the store house," he mumbled. "But here, in Tiphaine's own house—"

"You other folks," I said to them, "do you all want to stand round and watch me give Ottom another whipping, right here on your own dunghill? Say the word and it'll happen."

"Stand easy, Ottom," Tiphaine ordered him. "John, if you're not of us, who are you?"

"I keep a-telling you all," I said. "Just call me John."

Again I walked toward the door with my guitar. Not slow, not fast. I thought they teetered on their feet, but nair one of them followed. I went on along the hall, past that Earth Mother thing, and out the front door and along the bushy path, with scrapy noises to both sides. I got to the street and headed off for where my camp waited.

CHAPTER 6

So I slogged straight on ahead, on that gravel track, without much of a light from the veiled sky. The houses on both sides were dark, no lamps to be seen in the windows, though it wasn't much late in the night. I wondered what folks might could be up to inside, and I allowed to myself that likely it wasn't aught of good.

Back there behind me rose up a murmur of voices. I had a sense that the ones I'd seen in Tiphaine's house had come out to her gate. Maybe not all of them, but anyway some, to crane after me and chatter. Leastways, they didn't come along after me. Tiphaine had allowed that there was something about the trash fires that pestered them. And I was human enough to be glad for that.

On I went, and on, in what blurred moonlight there was. I left the houses of Wolver behind me on the road. Yonder stood that ruined-down old church, all among its brushy yard and its tipped-over gravestones. It looked dark and sad in the night; and no wonder, a-being forsaken thattaway. Once it had tried to serve the town of Wolver with the good word, and now it was long gone past such work.

I felt some better when I got past that church and had the settlement of Wolver, with all those lost and lurking folks, behind me. There was a sense in me that I'd be better off away from Wolver. "Our will is here expressed," Tiphaine had said at her table, and had added on that their will would get to be in other places. But not right yet, I let myself hope.

The way was darker there, with the trees to both sides of

the track, but I'd been along there by daylight four–five times. I let my feet find their direction, the way you can do with a good, smart horse in the nighttime. They took me off the road and into the woods at the right place. I made it my business not to trip over roots till I got to my camping place.

I leaned my guitar against a yew tree out of sight of whatever might could have tried to come a-following on. Then I sat down on the hump of a root. I didn't make a fire, that would attract attention. I reckoned it was high time to think things out, think them out clear and correct.

There was no I reckon about it, Tiphaine and her crowd had made them a long jump to what they thought was a fact and wasn't a fact, no such thing. I'd come into Wolver past the junk heaps and the fires they seemed somehow to be afraid of, and then I'd whipped Ottom Orcutt in a fistfight when he wasn't supposed to be whipped. After that, Tiphaine had taken her try at me to have me kiss the foot of her Earth Mother statue, and I hadn't, and that made her more certain. She and her crowd had been ready to put me through some sort of initiation, and I'd sung them that Witch of Wokey song to show them there was nothing doing.

So now, I reckoned they'd put me down as their enemy, which was just what I was. They hadn't come a-following after me—it might could be that they worried about the fires at the trash dumps, for whatever it was scared them about those. But I'd done well not to hang round in Wolver and bother them. Anyhow, I had found out what they were up to. Witchcraft, that was what, and I could report that fact to the government men.

But what would the government men say to that?

No great much, I reckoned, and what they would say would come with a dry grin. Witchcraft? Go tell about it to the little baby children, and don't bother us about it unless your witchcraft is a-doing something actual. That was more or less what they'd say, and then they'd add on something like, what you'd better do, John, is just pick your guitar and sing us a couple–three verses of "Old Mountain Dew."

After all, they'd have something on their side of what the Cherokees call *tum-tum*. Up to now, Tiphaine and her crowd had put on a show with me, and no more than that. Their powers, if they had them, hadn't worked. Ottom Orcutt had been supposed to give me a whipping, and it had gone the other way round. Tiphaine had been supposed to spellbind me with her pearl ring, and it hadn't come off. Maybe all they had was just crazy talk, stuff that wasn't so.

But I doubted that. I had a feeling that there was something big and ugly here, and I've learned to hark at my own feelings. I'd go back to Wolver in the morning, even if they were set for me, were fixing to do something rough to me. It would likely be dangerous, but danger had been my breakfast and dinner and supper before this. I'd better do it. Smell out their secret, see for sure how bad a thing it was. You don't report just guesses to the government. You report facts, or no point a-making a report.

The night was airish and I felt some touch of cold, but I didn't make me a fire. Nobody had followed me on to my camp so far, but this might could be the time for somebody to try it. I leant myself to the yew tree beside my guitar and sort of shrugged my clothes round me. That helped some. I'd had me a day to tire the strongest man ever was, and so I don't much reckon it was strange for me to go off to sleep, with a whippoorwill a-piping the three notes of its call to me.

I don't truly reckon that the sleep I slept was air kind of a sound one. I had me a set of dreams that made me start awake time after time. Once I thought I was out a-walking with Evadare along a path, when a big black dog jumped up right in front of us and showed us fire a-blazing out of its mouth. Then again, it seemed like as if I stood beside a foggy river and watched a big boatload of folks as they sank down

into black water. Finally I thought I could hear voices all together, and when I waked up from that I truly heard them.

They were someway far off, I knew the second I heard
them in the night, somewhere off toward Wolver. They
sounded like a bunch of men and women a-laughing and a-
hollering all together, and I stood up so as to hear them better. There came a long-drawn strain of music, shrill and trembly. I wondered myself what instrument made it. After that,
they seemed to start in to sing together. The Wolver crowd
was up to something, that was for sure, far off but within
earshot.

I pulled out from under the yew tree and looked up at the
sky. I could barely see the stars, but there were enough of
them to tell me it was in the small hours before morning. I
told myself that it was up to me to go have a look.

Careful as careful, I picked my way out to the road and
faced toward where the noise was. Above me was the veiled
half of the moon, and as I moved on the road I hung close to
the trees at the side so as to stay out of the soft light. The
noise got louder yet as I made my way nearer. Finally I came
to where I could see to the tumbledown church, and that's
where they were.

Yonder stood the church, a-looking all haggly and ruined,
even in the murky moonlight, and amongst the bushes in the
yard there blazed up a fire. Maybe they'd put something into
that fire, because it flung up streaks of white and blue
amongst the red, like something I'd once seen when the
northern lights were out.

And an almighty racket went up from there round the fire,
those chanty voices and the shrill, wailing music.

I kept a-sneaking along the side of the road, as close under
the trees as I could get. Now I made out black shadows on
the jump, betwixt the fire and me. Those were folks at some
kind of dance, and as I made my way still yet closer under

the trees, I could see that they looked to be naked. By then I
could hear the things they whooped out:

"Hyaa, hyaa!"

"Sabbat, sabbat!"

"Dance here, dance there!"

It was more or less a song, and it got to my recollection of
things I'd heard and read about. That was the way witches
yelled to one another at their ceremonies. I was getting in on
a big Satan-worshipping business, as if I couldn't have
guessed at such a thing already.

But me, I needed to get a closer look than I had under the
trees. While they sang and danced, I flung myself down
where a shadow went across the road and wiggled my way
over like a worm. On the far side I hiked up on my hands
and knees and crawled toward the bushes in front of the
burying ground.

I could see them plain in the firelight. Men and women
two by two, as naked as they were born on this earth, and I
might say that no great many of them looked at all good
thattaway. They moved in front of the fire from my left to
my right, the widdershins way. I saw them do a few steps
with each couple back to back, the figure the dance-callers
call do-si-do, now stooped almost to the ground, now straight
up with hair a-flying and a-whipping in the air. And on the
far side of the fire, in the middle of the circle of dancers,
stood what looked like three others of them, straight and
motionless as rocks.

I reckoned I'd better find out what that three was up to
while the others danced. The thing to do was get round to
their side of the fire.

I'd put myself all the way into the burying ground by now,
and I crawled amongst old gravestones with that music a-
making its whine all round. By that time, I could see the
folks who were a-making it. A man and a woman, and he had

an accordion and she had some kind of flute or fife. I wondered myself if I could pick that wild-as-all-hell tune on my guitar. The musicians stood off to the side away from the dancing circle, and I crept on my all fours behind them. There rose up the church, the closest I'd seen it. It was that busted to pieces, I wouldn't have wondered at it if it had fallen down before my eyes. I got to it, almost to where it had the remains of steps, and from there I could see into the circle, could see the three by the fire.

And then, as I'd found my way to the far side of the fire, those naked folks switched off to dance round in a line, one behind the other. The flute and the accordion player did a new tune and all of them sang to it, something like this:

> Cummer, go ye before, cummer, go ye;
> Gif ye not go before, cummer, let me!

I'd nair heard that sung before, but once I'd read it, and it was the song that once got sung for just such a dance as this, long ago in Scotland at another torn-down old church, at North Berwick. Just what the words meant I couldn't tell, but they made my blood grow chill in me.

From where I'd dragged myself to spy, I could see past the dancers into the space round the fire. Of the three that stood there, two were dressed up someway crazy. One was a tall figure, robed all dark, with horns on the head, like the ones on the Earth Mother's head in Tiphaine's hall. The other, not so tall, had a sparkly head ring like a crown, and a robe of red. The third of them I knew, for she stood all pale-white naked and right shapely, with her yellow hair in a tumble. It was the young girl Lute Baynor, and seemed like to me that she shivered.

"And now!" they all yelled out together. "And now, our father who wert in heaven!"

Wert in heaven . . . who was it had been in heaven and fell out? I recollected that, too.

The two robed ones were up to something near the fire. They had two rocks there, and they were a-putting something across them. It was a sort of flat slab, maybe one of the tombstones, and they laid it the way you put a board on trestles to make a picnic table. The one in red took Lute Baynor by the wrist and sort of pulled her along, and she lay down on her back on the flat rock. Then the red-robed one stood over her and put a tall cup, silver by the look, on her white belly. It was the kind of cup you use for a communion ceremony. They were just before a-having some kind of special do, what you call a ritual, and I could reckon it would be a right ugly one.

I got up on my hands to see if I could make out what was a-going on. And that was my mistake.

"A stranger!" whooped the one in the dark robe with the horned head, and I knew the voice. Tiphaine, that was what voice.

"A spy!" she called out in that ringing voice of hers. "There by the steps—capture him!"

That quick, they were after me. All the men of the bunch, eight or ten of them, naked and fast on their feet.

I wasn't about to fight them all, not that many. I jumped to my feet and ran myself, straight at them. They weren't set for that to happen, and I sailed right through amongst them. One tried to get a hand on me, but I knocked him sideways with an elbow. I tore on into where the dancing circle had been—only a bunch of women there, with their clothes off and their hair straggly, all a-goggling—and I tore past that altar. Lute Baynor sat up and knocked over the silver cup. I jumped high at the fire and through it, felt its heat on me for a wink of time. I landed at a run on the far side, and at a run I went a-sailing off to get out of the churchyard amongst the old stones of the grave.

All those men were after me, a-yelling to one another. "Catch him!"

"Is that John?"

"Get him, drag him down!"

I wove my way through some scratchy, thorny bushes and was out on the gravelly road. I headed in the direction away from Wolver. They came on behind me, a-yelling. I heard one of them come out with a bad word, likely his bare foot had come down on a sharp rock. But another of them was close at my back, I could tell and nair needed to look round over my shoulder. All of a sudden quick, I turned back to face him because I had to.

"I've got him!" the naked man yelled as we came together.

He wasn't big, that's how come him to run ahead of the others. I saw the white of his eye shine out in the dark. I just put out my fist and let him rush in against it, and I felt it smack the bones of his face. Over he went, flat down. Then the others were up to me, all round me, all over me.

They all of them seemed to be a-hitting me at once. I hit back my best. I picked out the biggest of them—it was Ottom Orcutt, I saw right off, all humped over with muscle under his hairy hide. I speared him straight in the middle of the mouth and then fetched over my right, rockabye, on his ear, and put two more into his belly while he staggered. I felt him wilt down with it, but meantime those others were a-punching at me, a-kicking at me. I tried to fight all of them at once, the best I could, but I couldn't, even with that first fellow down and out and Ottom limped over on one knee. Another of them sort of spun down, I don't recollect how I hit him to make him fall. My head rang and echoed with fists a-landing against it. Then one of them clubbed me from behind, with maybe a chunk of wood.

All of a sudden I was down, too, down on the gravel, and I thought it would feel right good to lie there, but I mustn't. I rolled over and tried to get up, and meanwhile their naked feet were a-slogging me in the ribs, the back. It was just no use to try to get up against all that. They were all a-kicking me when I was down, and dimly I wondered myself if they'd let me live long enough to be fetched back to where Tiphaine waited.

"We've done his business for him," wheezed a voice over me.

Then through the night came the long, throaty crow of a rooster.

"Hark at that!" said another of them. "Let's get out of here!"

Next second they were all gone from round me. No more kicks. I lay there, sort of dim and dreamy in my mind. From off where my wits had halfway pulled themselves to, came a memory of another old saying; that worshippers of the devil can't abide a cock crow.

My head jangled like a rung bell. I began to hurt all through me. I rolled over again and tried to shove a knee under me.

"Take it easy," said a quiet bass voice, near at hand.

A touch on me. I got myself together enough to wiggle clear from it. I hiked up on my knees, then onto my feet, to fight again if I had to, but it was too much to do. Down I went on a knee again.

"I'm a friend," said the bass voice. "I want to help you."

A hand came down under my arm, to hoist me up. I couldn't have stood up if whoever it was hadn't held me on my feet.

"Let's go," he said.

I sort of stumbled and staggered my way along. I couldn't see, and my head howled. I wondered myself where I was a-being taken to, and if I could make it.

CHAPTER 7

Likely I more or less went blank in my mind for a while, but I must have kept my feet on the move under me somehow, with that deep-voiced fellow a-holding me up onto them, with his arm round me. There come up times when you can do the like of that without air sure way of aught to tell you you can. I don't reckon I saw a great much in the dark, nor either felt much. I just moved along some way or other, with the man's help. And at last, finally at last, he got me to where we were to make our stop.

Nor do I recollect how come me to lay myself down. Like as not, I was too far gone by then to know for sure. And I knew not a thing else, not even dreams. Not till at last I waked up and felt hurty all over me.

"Let's hope you'll be feeling some better today," said that same deep voice that had spoken to me the night before. "Here, how'd you like to have a slug of coffee?"

I dragged my eyes open. I lay flat on my back on some sort of bed, and I had on all my clothes except for my boots—he must have dragged them off me. The room had walls of up and down plank, turned brown with years of time. I smelt a tangy smell, what I figured to be cedar twigs in a fire somewhere. Over me leant the man with the voice, a big blue-enamel mug in his hand. His other hand hiked my head up so that I could drink. That was stout, black coffee, as hot as I could well stand, and it seemed like as if it climbed all through me and helped me to where I had the strength to sit up. I caught my breath, for it hurt to move.

"You had you a right bad beating," said his deep voice. "They were more or less five-timing you."

"They sure God were," I agreed him.

"But it won't help you to swear about it," he said, and that was true, naturally. "Anyhow, I don't reckon you're at all bad hurt inside you. I sort of examined you all over while you lay there. No broken ribs or like that, though it's natural you're right much bruised."

I looked at him. He was a black man, and I mean truly black. His strong, smooth-shaved face looked as you see on an old bronze statue somewhere in a town square. Wrinkles were crossed back and forth into it. He appeared to me like as if he'd had some hard fight with life and had come out the winner in it, and maybe got himself hurt some in the winning. Up above his face, his hair was balded out in front, and it was cut short on the sides. It lay against his head in tight little kinks, like the steel wool you use to scrub out a pot. He wore an old surplus army shirt, patterned with green leaves stamped into the cloth, and khaki pants. His shoulders looked square, and his hands were big. He wouldn't be as tall as I am, but still a good height for a man, better than the average. And I reckoned him for someone in his middle years, not right young but not old, either.

"Whatever time of day has it got to be?" I inquired him.

He dug out a big round pocket watch, like what railroad conductors used to carry. "It's on about a quarter to three in the evening. You've had near twelve hours of sleep, and it appears to have done you some good."

The sound of his voice showed he was black, and he talked like somebody with education; more education than I have.

"I've sure enough got to thank you for a-saving me from them that were all fixed to stomp me to pieces," I said, with a twinge of my hurt ribs to remind me.

He grinned just a line, and shook his wise-looking head.

"Don't credit me with so much," he said. "If you've got to

thank somebody, thank that old rooster that crowed out so loud in the dark, hours before his usual time. Because a rooster's crow scares them and all their spooky kind, puts into them the fear of the God they say they don't believe in."

That figured. I thought back on an old, old ballad about ghosts:

> Then up and crowed the red, red cock,
> And up and crowed the gray;
> The oldest to the youngest said,
> "It's time we were away."

"All right, but you got me here somehow and took care of me somehow," I said. "I'd be proud to shake your hand for that."

"And I'd be proud to shake yours." He gave me his broad, dark, long-fingered hand.

"My name's John," I said. "Folks just call me John."

"And I'm Simon Latchney. You can call me Simon."

All the time we'd been talking, I'd taken the chance to see the place where Simon Latchney had fetched me. It was cabin-sized, a room with plank walls the way I've said, and two little glassed windows, just now raised up, and a half-open door. Put center of one side wall was a fireplace of sooty brick, with cedar scrub a-burning in it. Across the room were set a table and two old chairs, and on the table one of those hot plate cooking things that work off a tank of oil. On the fireboard above the hearth stood a few books and a kerosene lamp. An open cupboard in a corner had canned stuff on its shelves, and there were white potatoes in a bucket next to the cupboard.

The bed I sprawled on was an old iron cot, covered with an olive drab blanket that must have dated all the way back to the war, washed and sun-roasted time after time till it was faded. The pillow had an old Union Mills flour sack for a slip. I made myself shove up till I sat on the edge of the bed.

"Look here, Simon," I said, "you must have put me to bed in the only bed you have. What did you do, sleep on the floor?"

"No, John, not on the floor. I sat up in the chair yonder, I'd sleep a little bit and wake up a little bit. I harked at you, and you were sort of mumbling to yourself. Finally you did drop off, and so did I."

All the time he talked, he was busy a-cooking something on the hot plate.

"I'm purely a nuisance to you," I said.

"No, you needed help. You're a man and a brother. I help such when I can manage, and glad to be able."

"Hark at me, Simon, I'm not about to lie here and hog the one bed you have." I tried to get to my feet, but I hurt all over and sat back down again. "Out yonder, somewhere or other in the woods round about here, I've got my camping stuff—blankets and clothes and, sure enough, my old silver-strung guitar. Let me get my feet under me and I'll go look for them."

But his strong, dark hand held me back where I was a-sitting. "Nothing doing, John," he said, deep and quiet. "You'll need to loosen yourself up a whole lot before you try to go outdoors. Anyway, I've seen where you've been heading into those woods. You just let me wag your stuff back here. Right now, you couldn't travel twenty steps, the shape you're in."

He dished up a plateful of food from the pan. "Here," he said, and he fetched it back to me. "Eat on this. I'll pour you another fill of this coffee, too. Then I'll go out, be back directly."

He set the plate and cup on the blanket beside me, and smiled again and went out. The door swung shut behind him.

What he'd fixed for me was hot rice with bits of good-tasting smoked fish stirred all through it, with pepper and salt. Kedgeree, I've heard such a thing called by an English fellow I knew once. It ate right good, gentlemen, and that second

cup of coffee was as stout as the first. When I'd finished, I
felt a little bitty bit more like a man. I tried to get up again,
and that time I made it.

I tell you, I ached and hurt along both my sides and up my
back and down both my legs. But I sort of hobbled to where
I could put the plate and cup on the table, then to where I
could look out at a front window. I leaned my hands on the
sill to ease off on the places I felt hacked and bruised, and
studied the world outside.

Right off at once, I could see that the cabin was somewhere amongst those heaps and strews of trash on the road-
way into Wolver. I made out some sooty smoke from a pit,
with several smashed-up old cars next to it. Then this place
must be the same one I'd made out right on my first day a-
walking in, and it sure enough had to be Simon Latchney
who'd waved me a friendly hand that time. No wonder, then,
he burned those cedar branches in his fireplace, to kill out all
the smells from the trash. I leaned close against the pane, and
off one way I saw another place where smoke curled up.
Straight ahead of where I stood to look out was the road into
Wolver, to go along betwixt the thickets of dark trees. Simon
Latchney, then, was the fellow who looked after these
dumps.

Into my mind came another of those books I'd read and
studied in before I'd come to Wolver, a right scary book
about happenings even more creepy than what seemed to be
in the works amongst that sorry crowd in Wolver. There'd
been a garbage man in that tale, and as I figured he wasn't by
any stretch what you'd call a good citizen. He wound up with
something downright devilish a-killing him by drinking the
hot blood out of him, which meant that he got to be a blood
drinker, too. The fellow who wrote that book meant to scare
you with every page, and I'm honest to tell you he knew how
to do it. I've got to own up that to recollect it gave me a
crawly feeling all over my hurting body. But right off, I

thought of something else. I did my shaky hobble across the room to Simon's fireboard shelf.

Sure enough, amongst the books on it was a Bible bound in black leather, and it looked worn the way you'd guess it had been read through and read through a many times. It was sort of silly, then, to think that a vampire man would have that sort of holy book before him. If Simon studied in the Bible, he was bound to get something out of it. I took that Bible down and made my sore, careful way back to sit on the side of the bed, and flung open the cover.

On the front leaf inside was written, in ink: *Rev. Simon Latchney*, with a date about fifty-some years back that likely meant the day he was born. Below that: *Married Leona Deslow*, with another date for their marriage time, and then below that: *Leona died, age 42. And I will dwell in the house of the Lord forever.*

No more of the pen-and-ink writing than that, but it was enough to make me feel easy again. It told you a great big lot if you could put the twos together with the other twos. Simon, who'd fetched me to his house to look after me, was a preacher man, and when his wife had died he'd put down for her a text from what I reckon is the best known of all the Psalms of David. That should ought to be proof enough for me that Simon was all right, a good man, somebody to trust in air thing that came up.

I sat and looked on through his worn, old Bible, a-reading one part and then another that I've always liked, and that's how I put in my time till Simon came back in at the door, all loaded down with the stuff he'd found. He flung it down into the corner by the cupboard and slanted his eyes to study me.

"You seem to feel some better, John."

"Just a little some," I allowed.

"That's a right good book you got there. Good for you, for all men on earth, to read in."

"I've always liked it," I told him. "It says here in the front that you preach the good word."

"I used to, once." He sat down in a chair and got a corncob pipe out of his pants pocket and filled it from a tobacco can on the table. He struck a match to it. "I reckon I could still preach, I wasn't ever unordained from it. Back yonder, before this kind of folks took over in Wolver, the mill ran right big and had jobs for a right many people. Some of the workers were black, and I used to preach to them of a Sunday, this house or that. Then the new bunch came in and took over. The black folks all left out for other parts of the country. I hold my job here, I'm custodian of the county trash dump."

"County trash dump," I repeated after him. "That means, the county runs it, not Wolver."

"No, not Wolver. That range of folks would just as soon not come over this direction. They don't even use this road, they made themselves one of their own, down there along the river. They stay away from here on account of my fires."

"Yes, I looked out just now and saw them a-burning here and yonder. But why should they scare out the Wolver bunch?"

"Because," he said, "I set them for the Beltane time of the year, and then I never let them go out. I keep them going all the year round. But likely you don't know about Beltane."

I allowed I'd only heard the word, and he filled me in.

Way back on the ancient times, the way he told me—and he'd read all about it in the *Golden Bough* book—peoples of different countries built the Beltane fires on the night of May Day, to scare off all kinds of bad magic from their homes and fields. Another word for it was needfire, I didn't exactly understand what that meant, unless because it was needed. You had to start it the way fires were started long back before history began, the way old Indian tribes and other peoples did, with rubbing sticks.

I'd nair seen such a fire-making way, and Simon fetched his rubbing-stick gear out from a box under the bed to show me. There was a springy bow—yew wood, I saw—with a loose string, and a pointed spindle made out of a round twig of oak kind of like an arrow, and a sort of flat hearth of soft wood with charred notches in one edge. You had to have a tuft of tinder ready—what Simon pulled out of a little leather poke was dried-out moss, mixed with cedar shavings. When the heat of the spindle turned on the hearth made a little burning coal, the tinder was held to it to catch and blaze up. Then it was fed with twigs and splinters till it could handle air fuel you cared to put to it.

I wanted to work the thing, see how it fired up, but Simon put it all away again. It was just for the Beltane fires on the right day of the year, he said, and that made sense.

"That's how I do things here and there, on a May Day night," Simon finished his talk about it. "Not just one fire, but maybe half a dozen, all over this trash dump. And there's this difference about my Beltane fires, I don't let them go out, not from one May Day to the next. I feed them all the time, keep them on the burn, for what they can do to keep the Wolver kind of trash out. Rainy and snowy nights I'm sometimes out there for hours, hard at the job."

"But you're a preacher," I reminded him. "Do you sure enough believe in what you say is an old heathen way of fighting off magic?"

He just grinned over that. "Yes, I'm a preacher all right, but the good Lord hasn't yet appeared to tell me to overlook a bet. You look at my other books on the shelf yonder, you'll find the Talmud and the Koran and the Analects of Confucius."

"Do you hold with all those faiths, Simon?"

"Now you're trying to make me sound polytheistic. The only thing I figure is, there may be many ways to reach and serve the truth and the good."

"Sure enough," I said, "we won't quarrel about that."

"Anyhow, the Beltane fires I keep bright do help to scare the Wolver folks off from here."

"And how do those folks act with you?" I inquired him, but he only shook his head.

"I don't go into Wolver at all. I walk all the way to the county seat for what supplies I need. And Wolver doesn't take note of me, no note whatever. I'm black, you see, and they don't figure aught of use in me. Which suits me to a T. On my part, I reckon I feel sorry for them, or for anybody else so mixed up about life and truth, but I can't find it in my heart to value them a nickel's worth."

Simon didn't smile that time when he said it. Fact was, he looked right stern and grim. I reckoned it would be a good thing to change the subject, so I hiked myself up on my feet and drilled round the floor a few steps.

"It hurts all over but it's good for me to make a move," I said. "Now, tonight I'll unroll my bedding and sleep yonder by the fireplace."

"Before that, let me make you some kind of mattress out of cedar tips. And I won't take no for an answer."

"The thought of saying no didn't come to me for a second." I looked at my camping stuff, with the guitar a-leaning on top of it. "You know, Simon, you must be a good trailer to study out where I went into the woods and where I'd put my things."

"Oh," he said, a-drawing on his corncob pipe. "I watched you go in the first time you walked past. And that night, I went over there to have a look at you while you slept."

I sat down in the other chair. "Were those your tracks?"

"Sure enough. What makes you stare like that, John?"

I took in a deep breath. "I'm a-beginning to wonder if those devil worshippers aren't just gone gumps. If they don't have air power at all. Maybe I'm a-looking for the wrong bug under the stone."

CHAPTER 8

Simon sort of crinkled his brows and looked hard at me. "Whatever are you getting at, John? What's biting you?"

"It was you all the time," I said. "Out yonder at my camp, while I was a-laying myself down asleep."

"I've already told you that. I was there, all right, but I never did you aught of harm. What's to bother you about that?"

It was my turn to squinch up my own face. "I couldn't figure on those tracks I saw the first morning. I reckon I put them down for some kind of spy-thing from Wolver, there to look on me."

"Oh, no, John." He shook his head. "I've explained how they don't come this way much. They're scared of my fires."

And he had mentioned that about the fires, and so, I recollected, had Tiphaine.

"All right," I argued him, "if not one of them, I figured it might could be some creature they might send out for a spy. That was my chief notion."

"That church is as far as they ever come," he said. "When they chased after you last night, they must have been scared to do even that. And they'd have never dared to come as close as that camp you made."

"I wasn't thinking of human spies."

He grinned then. "Like a Bigfoot, a Sasquatch, the like of that? But nothing they might command would dare come if that devil crowd didn't dare. No, John, it was nothing but me. And I'm your friend, John."

I knew he said the truth about that. I tried to make him understand what was on my mind, while I tried to make myself understand it.

"Hark at me, Simon, I jumped to a conclusion when I woke up and saw your tracks. I set them down for something unnatural, and I more or less went a-walking into Wolver with that notion. Now, I begin to wonder myself if Wolver's plumb unnatural. I'd like you to tell me all you know about Wolver."

"I'll do that, but first off I'll set us another pot of coffee on to boil."

He lighted up the hot plate and set the pot on. Then he sat down again and talked about Wolver. Some things he said were new to me, others I more or less knew already.

In the years before, he said, the mill there had made money with fabrics woven of good mountain wool, and its owners had hired some black men and women to work in it. Simon came there for a job when his wife died, and he'd worked at a loom and also had preached to his friends of a Sunday, had done weddings for young lovers and baptized baby children. The church I'd seen and figured on wasn't ruined then, and services were held there for the white folks in Wolver. But then the mill business had gone bad, and a bunch of outlanders came in and bought it for near about nothing. That, said Simon, was round about seven years back. The first thing the outlanders did was let all the black workers go and put in a staff of their own crowd, to make labels.

"And just about that same time, Satan came to be worshipped hereabouts," said Simon. "The whole town was purely taken over by the devil crowd. All who didn't rightly belong to that brand of worship moved off away, blacks and whites both."

"Except you," I said.

"Except me. I was left all alone in the world, no wife, no children, and I decided I might do well if I stayed and kept my eye on things hereabouts. So I went into the county seat and got me this job to look after the county trash dump. I keep watch the best I can. That's all I've been able to do."

"I reckon I poked in here to keep watch, too," I said.

The coffee was done, and he filled the mugs for both of us. "Now," he said. "I've told you more or less about myself, and I'd suggest it's your time to tell me about yourself."

So I told him a little small bit about myself.

Naturally, I didn't name aught to him about how I'd been sent to Wolver nor yet who it was who'd done the sending. First I narrated about my young orphan days, how I'd learned to pick the guitar and how, here and there and yonder, learned to make the fight against evil. I mentioned Evadare, the one I loved, and how I'd met her. I told him two–three scary things that had happened to me in past times, such as like the Ugly Bird and the desrick on Yandro, like when Old Devlins Hatfield came back from his rest in the grave when his great-grandson called his name. Then about the rough, rough night I'd spent on Wolter mountaintop to settle accounts fairly with a couple of mean Druid brothers; and how the Shonokin people had come out from the place they kept their hiding to make their move, and hadn't got it done.

"I'd say that you have the heart and soul to stand against evil, John," said Simon as he listened.

Then I went on to tell how, lately, I'd fared in Wolver, how that place looked in its homes and yards; how I'd whipped Ottom Orcutt in a more or less fair fight when he had some kind of spell against a-being whipped; how Tiphaine, so sure of herself in that fine big house of hers, hadn't been able to run air charm on me with her pearl ring; and so on. Simon harked at all I said with the closest attention a man could call for.

"So," I said at the end of it, "what it looks like to me is, these charms they think they have aren't charms, no such a thing. Ottom just thought he was a master fighter, Tiphaine just thought she could witch my senses out of me. If they just thought it, there's no Satan power in Wolver. Just a bunch of gone gumps, a-fooling nobody but their own selves."

"I still hold that you've got a power of your own, against them," said Simon back. "John, if you tumbled right down to the pit below the bottom floor of hell, you'd come up again without a burn on you." He thought that over. "So far, anyway," he added on.

"Then how about the way I got myself beat on and kicked round last night?" I wondered, and twisted myself to see did I still hurt as bad as before.

"From what I saw of it at the time, that was a different thing altogether," he replied me. "That was just a plain gang-up on you, five or so against just you, like what could happen in an alley or a vacant lot in some mean town. It's a good job that old rooster crowed when he did, a good long way before his usual sunup. That helps prove my point. The crow of a rooster is a noise that evil things somehow can't stand."

"How come you to believe that?" I asked.

"Let me quote you something on the subject."

He thought a second, then he recited some poetry:

> The cock, that is the trumpet of the morn,
> Doth with his lofty and shrill-sounding throat
> Awake the god of day, and at his warning,
> Whether in sea or fire, in earth or air,
> The extravagant and erring spirit hies
> To his confines: and of the truth herein
> This present object made probation.

"That's from Shakespeare," I said. "*Hamlet*. I saw that play one time, at Flornoy College."

"Shakespeare knew a thing or two," said Simon, and quoted us some more:

And then, they say, no spirit dare walk abroad,
The nights are wholesome, then no planets strike,
No fairy takes, nor witch hath power to charm,
So hallow'd and so gracious is the time.

He'd said it off right well. "I was lucky," I allowed, "that that same old rooster let off with his crow, when the night wasn't yet done."

"That's another thing that helps my point," said Simon. "He crowed when you needed him. I'd reckon that there's still something with them when they try to magic you, spook you, and that can be put down. Some way or other, you're able to fight against such a thing. From what you've told me about yourself, I'd say you'd done it so many times in the past, you're what might be called sort of inoculated against those things."

It wasn't at all the first time I'd heard such a notion about me, and, to say the naked truth, I'd now and then reckoned it was so. It comforted me to hope that. Simon went over to the fire and put on a couple of chunks of hard wood, then some tufts of cedar needles on top.

"That keeps my house smelling good," he allowed.

"It might could do more than just that," I told him. "The Cherokees used to burn cedar branches to keep off ghosts and bad spirits. Though I notice that Tiphaine has a cedar hedge in front of her place."

"Does she burn it?"

"That I don't rightly know," I said.

"Speaking of the Cherokees, pull off your shirt and I'll give you some homemade Cherokee lotion to rub on those hurt places."

When I peeled down to the waist, I saw the bruises made

big dark splotches and oozy scrapes all along my ribs and on my arms and shoulders. I felt I could call myself lucky that those men had been barefoot, hadn't had on boots to put to me. Simon fetched me a bottle of brown liquid off one of his shelves, and I rubbed handfuls of it here and there, and right off quick I began to feel better. It looked to me like as if the dark bruises faded to brown and green, while I watched. I turned up my pant legs to rub more on my shins and knees where I felt the ache. Simon told me the lotion was something the Cherokee medicine men had learnt to boil up from different flowers and seeds and leaves, all stewed together to make a thick sort of tea.

"For one thing," he said, "there are the mashed-up seeds of viper's bugloss in that preparation. And for another, the juice of campion."

"Viper's bugloss," I repeated him, while I put on my shirt again. "And campion, so I've heard tell, was named rattlesnake weed by the Indians. Sounds another sight more like something to cure the bites of bad snakes than to cure sore muscles."

"For all I know, it might be good for snakebite, too. But for what's ailing you, how does it work?"

"It works fine," I said, and it sure enough did. I got up from where I sat on the bed and walked to test myself. I felt a whole lot more like my own man. Simon's lotion was a-working wonders, just in a few minutes, and no I reckon about it. I felt grateful as I buttoned up my shirt, and I said so.

"Which makes me grateful, too," he nodded. "Grateful that you're here, because I'd puzzled for years over what I could possibly do about what they're up to in Wolver. But now I've got you with me, maybe something will be done."

I hoped in my soul that he was right.

I felt good enough by then to be right glad to have my old guitar back, safe and sound. It had long been a good friend to

me, a comfort and a help in a many places. I picked it up and
tuned the silver strings and tried a chord or two. Simon
inquired me did I know some of the old hymns, so I hit the
tune out for one, and sang it:

> Lights in the valley outshine the sun,
> Look away beyond the blue . . .

He joined in with me to sing the deep harmony to that,
and his singing voice was a right good one, same as his talking voice. He called for another hymn by the name, and I
knew it well, so I picked that one, too:

> A few more steps to travel on,
> A few more days and I'll be gone;
> The River Jordan is dark and cold,
> It chills the body but not the soul.

"I swanny, Simon, that's not what I'd pick for the right
hymn for you," I said when we'd both sung it to the end.
"You look to me to have long, strong life in you still."

"Who's going to know how long or how short his life's
going to be?" Simon said.

"I don't figure on you for a man who's scared to die,
Simon."

"No, sir, and I'm not scared. I don't especially want to die,
but when death comes, why, I won't be scared of it and I
hope I'll be ready for it."

"And I sure enough hope I can truthfully say the same." I
stretched my arms and legs as I sat, to feel how they came on.
"Anyhow, that medicine you gave me to rub on has sure
enough done its wonders. I'm a-feeling right good just now."
I stretched again. "A right much of the sore feeling is gone
out of all those kicked and punched places. The Cherokees
knew what they were a-doing when they made that stuff."

"Then how would you like to go outside with me for a
spell and see how you fare?" he asked me.

"Why, I'd like that a whole lot." I fumbled on the floor for my boots and dragged them on.

"Good."

He went and picked up an ax from against the wall and headed for the door. He opened it a crack and peeked out.

"All's clear out yonder," he reported. "Not that I scarcely ever see folks from Wolver on the road."

The two of us stepped into the open. First thing I saw was a horseshoe nailed up over the door, toe down, rusty enough to show it had been there for years. A protection against evil, and I wasn't surprised to find it. Next thing I saw was shrubs a-growing in a line along the front of the cabin, and I stopped right there to have me a look at them. They were low and flat-topped, with crooked, thorny branches and heart-shaped leaves and little white flowers in close bunches.

"Hawthorn," I said. "Right pretty, too."

"I used to hear my old grandsire say it's a good protection against conjure stuff," said Simon. "That's why I planted it along there by the door."

We walked off along a path toward those dumps of trash. I looked back and made out a tree, a-growing high and round-topped behind the cabin. "Aspen," I said, and pointed at it.

"I like that to grow there, too," said Simon. "I've heard it claimed that the cross on Calvary was made of aspen."

I'd heard other claims about the wood of the cross. Among the trees it's reckoned to be made of are cedar, cypress, palm, olive, poplar, dogwood and so on. But I nair fetched it up. Instead of that, I looked up at the sky. Sure enough, that skin of mist was still over it, with the sun like a red-hot ball swaddled in it.

"Is the sky always like that, Simon?" I asked.

"It's been like that ever since that crowd took over in Wolver."

"What causes it to cloud up?"

"I don't know how to answer that."

Simon hiked the ax on his shoulder and led the way amongst grassy stretches and trash heaps to a deep pit where a fire smoked and smoldered in a whole mess of junky papers and rags and stuff. He wouldn't let me fool with the fire, but I borrowed the ax and wore down a dead hickory tree nearby and chopped it up into lengths. It made my muscles feel good to swing that ax. Simon fed the pieces into his fire where they would do the most good and last a spell.

"There," he allowed, "that looks to burn the whole day long and through the night till tomorrow."

We walked on away from the pit and dragged together wood enough to feed up another fire amongst some mossy-grown rocks. Along the road from the highway came a-rumbling a big truck loaded with garbage, and behind it was coupled on a rusty old dead automobile. It came into the trash area, and Simon went over to talk to the driver and his buddy. They dropped off the car amongst a clutter of others, and went beyond to dump the trash onto a heap where Simon showed them. The truck left out again and the two of us kept on with our tour round here and yonder.

In some places the garbage stunk to high heaven and the flies were thick, naturally. Birds settled one place another, to peck at what they could find to eat. I made out crows and blue jays and such as that, with, overhead, a big old buzzard with his wings reached all the way out to float on. The feathers at the ends of his wings looked like the spread-out fingers on two hands. Here and there through the dump areas were pools. Frogs sang in them, and hushed down when we tramped close to them. I kept a-looking up at the sky. I couldn't figure out how, without clouds bunched here or there, it could keep that dull look.

Simon built a couple more fires to burn up piles of the smelliest garbage. These weren't the sure-enough Beltane fires, he said, and he wouldn't try to keep them a-going all day and night and all year. I took note that he mourned, just a trifling bit, when we looked over the big bunches of dead automobiles, brought here and there and crowded up and left to rust away into nothing.

"I don't see why they don't tow those back out again, melt them down and use the iron in them some way," he said. "The day's apt to come when we run all out of iron, the same way we're running out of oil now. When all the iron's gone, mankind will have to go back to stone axes and chisels and bows and arrows."

"No more iron left?" I said. "That will be a long day a-coming."

"The longest day will come at last, John, and at the end of that longest day the end of the world will come."

Simon mostly wasn't pure down gloomy, but now and then he could sober your mind with such talk as that. I was right glad when he changed the subject and pointed me out some Turk's-cap lilies that grew in a moist little dip of the ground. It was a fairly good stand of them, with their purple-red flowers bunched at the tops of their stalks. The ground looked all scratched up round them. Simon nodded and allowed that, sure enough, he helped plants out, all sorts of places on that dump area. He'd even tote buckets of water to them, from the pools, in the dry times when he figured they needed it.

"Do these Turk's-caps help out against conjure magic?" I inquired him.

"Can't rightly say they do or they don't. But they help me out, just to study them now and then."

For, plain to see, he was a somebody who loved flowers, not just those like the hawthorns at the door of his cabin for what protection they might could give him.

"Yonder comes another truckload of trash," he said. "You sort of keep down out of sight, I'll go have a word with them."

I moved into a low place and watched through some

bushes as the truck wallowed in and Simon talked to the driver and pointed to where the stuff must be dumped. As the truck pulled out again, Simon came back to where I was.

"You're not the only stranger hereabouts, John," he said.

"What do you mean?"

"At the county seat, a car with a Washington city license checked in at the auto court this morning. Folks are a mite curious because the man won't say a word about what business he's come to do there."

"Is that a fact?" I said. "Here, Simon, I'm a-going into town."

"What for?" he asked me, with his eyes gone wide.

"Just call it curiosity," I said, and started for the road.

"Hold on now, you're sore from that fight you had," he called after me.

"No," I hollered him back over my shoulder. "I feel right good, that salve drove the sore plumb out of me."

"John—"

I didn't reply him air word more than that. I slogged off for where the highway would be.

A little sparrow lit on a bush and chirped at me. I studied on how sparrows would be thought pretty birds if we hadn't made up our minds they were pests. Then I realized that not once at air place close in to Wolver had I seen a bird or heard one sing.

CHAPTER 9

It wasn't so almighty far to the highway, and I walked it right fast. Almost as soon as I got to the edge of the pavement, along came a beat-up blue farm truck that stopped when I jabbed out with my thumb. A chunky old farmer said, "Get in, friend," and I did so. He started us up again. "I don't reckon as how I know you," he said. "You a stranger in these here parts?"

"Nair been to your county seat before," I replied him. "The only place hereabout I air heard tell of is called Wolver."

"Oh," he said, "them sorry Wolver folks. You ain't none of them, I dare hope."

"No, not me. I'm a stranger, the way you said, and I'm a-hoping to meet a fellow at the county seat. What sort of people are there in Wolver?"

He snorted his nose over that. "I don't see them much. They come in to shop. I take it they feel holy about something. You pull a tent canvas over Wolver, I reckon you'd have just one big crazy house. But they don't interest me no more than a dog a-running a fox up over the ridge." He thought about that a second. "Not as much," he amended it.

"Holy about something," I repeated him. "Some kind of religion?"

"That's what, but I don't rightly know about it. I do my own best to do right and look after myself. Ain't nobody air helped me aught in this life, and I don't truly reckon nobody air will."

"The man I'm a-meeting is supposed to be at a motor court in town," I changed the subject.

"There ain't but the one motor court, they call it the Trail Motel. It don't get much used, only when court sits twice a year. I'll drop you off there. Now, here we come into town."

It was no great thing for a county seat, I judged, maybe eleven hundred folks or so. The houses on the street were ordinary and quiet-looking, and so were folks a-walking along. At the center was the courthouse square, with a big yellow brick building in its middle. That courthouse looked smudged, and the farmer told me that over the years it had been on fire three times, only twice on purpose. Round the outside of the square were some store shops, a barbecue stand and a little bank building. There was likewise the jailhouse, and behind it the steeple of a church. Finally, a big sign, TRAIL MOTEL.

"There's the place you're a-looking for, friend," said the farmer, as he put on his brakes.

"I do thank you kindly."

"No, I was glad to have you along to talk to."

I looked at the Trail Motel. It was just a row of square little rooms painted blue and gray, with in front a broad paved strip and two–three cars parked there. I walked in back of those, and on one of them was a D.C. license. I headed for the room it was parked against, and knocked at the door.

Silence, time enough to take in a breath. Then the door opened a crack, for somebody to look out before opening it all the way.

"Yes?" said a man's voice. "What is it? Oh, you're John, aren't you? Come right in."

I stepped in across the threshold, and he closed the door again behind me, quick. We stood a-looking on one another. He was maybe somewhere in his thirties, a tad better than common tall, medium built, yellow curly hair and a square face and an all-business look about him. He was dressed all in different browns. His shirt was the color of clean sand, and it was open at the neck, with a chocolate-colored tie pulled loose. His pants were of good tan cloth. His shoes were deep brown and shiny. Yonder on a hook hung his jacket, two tones of brown. A nice-looking fellow, but naught special. Except for those clothes, which had likely cost hundreds of dollars all told, you'd see such like a man a-selling things in a store or maybe a-teaching in a high school.

"What brings you here, John?" he said. "How did you know I was here? Sit down and tell me."

I took a cushiony chair. The room wasn't big, but it was nice. A bed with a soft green spread, a desk with an open briefcase on it, a TV set, a bureau and a mirror. I looked all round it before I spoke back.

"I got a word about you, more or less secondhand," I said. "And what about what brings you here? Has Washington got to spy on me?"

"Washington does considerable spying, but not on you. I was sent because there's a trifle of worry in high places about you."

"Do tell," I said. "And you seem to know me, but I don't know you."

He took a wallet out of his hip pocket and showed me a stamped card with his photograph on it, likewise his name—but I'm not supposed to tell that name just now—and what was the bureau, or whatever it is, he worked for.

"I'd offer you a drink," he said, "but I don't drink myself, didn't bring anything drinkable. What have you to report so far?"

I sat and narrated all that had gone on with me, what Wolver folks had said and done and tried to do. I talked the most part about Tiphaine and Simon Latchney. The man had a pad of paper and pen, and made a heap of quick notes.

"Tiphaine," he repeated her name. "You make her sound lovely, in something of a forbidding way."

"Forbidding's the word," I said. "She's a right pretty woman, and a right smart one. Maybe she's got to be crazy in her line of business, but she's no way idiotic. None of the Wolver crowd is idiotic."

"No, sir," he agreed me there. "They have a sort of perverse rationality. But now, I said I came down here to see if you were all right. However, there also seems to be an interesting descent on Wolver in the works."

"What do you mean by that talk?"

He smiled a sort of secret smile. "As you probably know, sometimes it's hard for our service to investigate things. State and federal laws are strong on protecting all possible rights of people. Any people. We're discouraged from tapping telephone lines or jimmying open doors or looking at private correspondence—all that sort of thing. But we have our methods, as I believe Sherlock Holmes once said. And we've found out that Wolver will shortly be visited by people much more distinguished than you or I."

"I can't claim to be distinguished," I said.

"These gentlemen can. They happen to be special representatives of two important foreign governments."

I'm not allowed to name those governments, either, but take my oath for it, they're important. "What will they be up to in Wolver?" I wanted to know. "I've told you it isn't even a town, just a little settlement, with a few folks a-working at the old mill there; no mayor, no town board. Tiphaine seems to be able to tell air man, woman or child if they can walk or stay on base, and of course there's that belief they follow. But more than that, I can't call it much of a place for big foreign officer people to come a-visiting at. And I've still got it all to find out if the things that Tiphaine and her crowd claim are as bad and powerful as they're cracked up to be."

"You're so right." And he nodded his curly yellow head. "The First Amendment to the Constitution guarantees them —guarantees all people—the right to worship as they please.

This United States government was not organized on religious lines. I can quote you that First Amendment if you like."

"You don't have to," I said. "I can quote it myself."

"If their worship made them commit felonies, it would be different. In the past, we've investigated various cults for homicides and swindlings and misappropriation of funds. As it is—well, the United States government could be made to look very silly indeed by interfering with even the most bizarre style of worship. And it can't afford to be made to look any sillier than it looks at present."

"I won't quarrel with you about that," I said, and he laughed a quiet laugh.

"Yet the government remains as interested as when you were first asked to come to Wolver and find out what you could," he said.

"What's the government a-going to do with what I find out?"

"Nobody has, as yet, confided in me on that subject. I can only speak to the interest, and you already know about that. But this new development—these foreign visitors to Wolver— it's up to us to find out what they propose to do. I sit here and try to decide whether I'd not better go to Wolver myself."

"Don't you air think of such a thing," I said, quick as I could. "They're already strong on their guard there, and I don't know what they might could do to another stranger amongst them. You've caused you enough talk right here at the county seat. Folks wonder themselves what you're up to round here."

"Really? Then I must do something about that. I'll let it be known that I'm—let's see—I'm making some sort of real estate survey. I can talk real estate convincingly. But about Wolver—"

"You'd better leave that for me to handle," I said to him, while I wondered how I could handle it.

"I'll trust that part to you, then. I don't believe I could trust the assignment to a better man." He grinned over that. "But let's have this conference amount to something. Let's come to where a religion, even the worship of Satan according to apparently classical ritual, leaves off and crime begins. First and foremost, what crimes do these people commit? Human sacrifice? Murder?"

"Not that I've seen, not that I rightly know of," I said. "Though it's the naked truth that they acted like as if they wanted to kill me, till that old rooster crowed them off me just in the nick of time."

"Theft, then? Swindling? Blackmail?"

"There might could be those, but I nair came up against them so far. Still and all, I wonder myself how Tiphaine can have that fine big house and live and act like a queen on this earth, without money from somewhere."

"Subversion?" he inquired me next. "Treason?"

"If they could bring those off, yes. I'd say that was the main hold of their religion."

"Ah," he said, "here, at last, is where we get to a combination of worship and crime. As with that interesting religion of the East, Thuggee, which gave us a word of all work in criminology. And there have been various cults of human sacrifice, and the law of the land has cracked down on those. But we must have evidence of such things, not just prejudice. Prejudice is what sent Socrates and Jesus and many other good men to their deaths."

That made me recollect some things Tiphaine had said. "Since you've got your eye on Wolver," I said, "what have you all found out so far about Tiphaine and the others there?"

He got up and got his briefcase and took out some sheets of paper. They'd been typewritten on.

"We've traced a few things here and there," he said, a-reading at it. "For instance, that man Simon Latchney is in the clear. His record looks fine here—a combat veteran of World War Two, made sergeant and got a silver star; known as a minister and a charitable person; pays his taxes, votes, all those things. And here, we have Ottom Orcutt. He doesn't vote, he pays taxes under protest. Once he served time for making illegal whiskey."

"I've known good men who did that, and what they made was good," I felt I had to say. "What about Eula Jarboe and Quill Norbury?"

"Both those names are here on this list," he replied me, his finger on it. "Eula Jarboe has business with shippers of supplies for her store, but no deliveries come directly to her—she comes here to town to pick up her goods. She was married once, divorced after her husband quarreled with her and left her. Spent some time at the State Hospital for the Insane, was called cured and came to Wolver. Quill Norbury is from somewhere up North, was fired from a job in a textile factory, but seems to be a fairly good businessman and no particular file on him."

"Lute Baynor?" I said.

"Yes, here she is. Sometimes she comes into town, that's how we checked on her. She was a high school dropout, quarreled with her parents and left home. Thought she was smart to do that. Won't answer letters from her mother."

"And Tiphaine," I said the name. "What have you got on her?"

"Nothing," he said. "Not a damned thing."

"Why, now," I said, "she's the most important one in Wolver, man or woman. She purely runs that place—"

"Purely, you say?" he interrupted.

"You can excuse my country talk. I mean to say, she sure enough runs that place. There's not a soul dares get up in the morning or lie down at night without her word of leave."

"That's interesting," he said, "and, as I think, extremely important. But we haven't any information about who she is or what she does. Remember, we've had to find all our information from points outside Wolver. Not one operative has gone in until you were sent on special assignment."

"Tiphaine's quite some kind of name," I offered.

"The only Tiphaine I ever heard of was the wife of Bertrand du Guesclin, and he was a French hero of the Hundred Years War."

"Which was near about six centuries ago or better," I said.

"I keep marveling at your big fund of general information. Well, might that be your Tiphaine? After six centuries?"

I shook my head no. "She's not one of the walking dead, I vow. If she was to come into this room, and I hope she doesn't, you'd think she was alive, all right. Likewise, near about the prettiest woman you air saw in your life, in your dreams or out."

"I gathered as much, and you intrigue the hell out of me." He looked at me hard. "The logical explanation is, she wasn't born with the name of Tiphaine. Witches take new names."

"Lots of folks take new names."

"That's true. Trotsky was born Bronstein. Lenin was born, let's see, Ulyanov. Josev Dzhugashvili had the good sense to change his name to Stalin. And Mary Pickford was Gladys Smith to start with, and the Jones of John Paul Jones was a later addition."

"I'll find out about Tiphaine," I promised.

"I hope you can, for so far it all adds up to the fact that we don't have the evidence we need to go into Wolver."

"The evidence is there somewhere," I told him, and sounded stubborn in my own ears. "If I don't have the proof yet, I have my reasons."

"You have your suspicions," he corrected me. "We must expect more of you than those."

"Hell," I said, and thought how Simon wouldn't relish my

use of that word. "Hellfire, I expect more of myself than those." I got up. "Hark at me, this has been a good talk and I'm right glad you were interested enough to come round these parts. But me, I'd better study about a-getting back yonder."

"I'll drive you."

"Part of the way, maybe."

"And I'll be staying right here until I hear from you again," he promised. "I'll be the interested real estate opportunist. And I'm going to request more men to come into this area, at once." He grinned again. "As my real estate partners, perhaps. Or customers joining me here, that would be better. I'll see that the word gets around town to the effect."

"That should ought to do it," I granted him. "But just now, let me go out alone and get in your car. Then you wait maybe a minute or so, make sure nobody's got too much of an eye on us, and come out after me."

"John," he said, "you should be in government service."

"I reckoned I sort of was, more or less."

I went to the door, cracked it to look out, and stepped into the open. I went clear out to the street, then I headed back on the sidewalk next to the parking area until I came opposite the car with the D.C. license. I ducked in quick beside it and got in and waited. Pretty soon the fellow came out, strolled over and got in under the wheel. He started us up, backed out, and headed up the street and out of town.

"You make me feel like a coward," he allowed. "I mean, letting you go to Wolver alone."

"You stay out," I told him, like as if I had the order to give. "One stranger is about all they'll stand for at a time. You give me a week in there."

"If you're not out in a week," he said, "I'll come myself. It will be perfectly lawful to look for you if you're missing. And I won't come alone, either."

I reminded myself that when Tiphaine had threatened me,

I'd told her that there might could be good friends who'd come and seek out what had been done to me. Only she hadn't guessed that they'd be from the government.

We didn't take long to get to the place where that sorry side road led away toward Wolver. He stopped the car when I bade him, and I got out.

"You take care of yourself, John," he warned me.

"I aim to do that thing."

"Somehow, I believe you will."

He swung his car round to head back to the county seat. I walked in, as I'd walked on the first day.

It was familiar ground now, all the way along to the trash dumps, to the fires that burned on them, to Simon Latchney's cabin with those hawthorns in bloom round it. Before I could knock on the door, Simon had it open to me.

"I'm glad you're back," he said. "What were you up to in town?"

"I looked for that stranger who had the folks puzzled. He's told it that he's more or less a-looking at some real estate."

"You starting in to get hungry? Look, it's nearly evening."

So it was. The foggy sun was down to the tops of the mountains.

"Come on in. I've got some little scraps of meat I can do something with for us."

CHAPTER 10

I came in, and Simon shut the door and gave me a look.
"Whatever just did happen with you in town?" he said.
Instead of replying him right off, I looked to where, on the table next to the hot plate, there lay a little unwrapped package. Not enough pieces of red meat there to make a fair-sized fist.
"Why don't you let me try to fix us a supper one time?" I asked.
Simon smiled. "You're not going to talk about what went on in town, are you? Well, all right. If you want to cook, go on ahead. I'll step outside and cut some evergreen for your bed by the hearth."
He picked him up the ax and went out at the door, and I studied that little wad of beef he'd brought out for us to eat.
It looked barely enough for only just one man, and I studied on how to stretch it. I lighted the hot plate and put the beef scraps in a saucepan of water to heat up and get tender. While I waited, I looked through the potato bucket for a great big one and I peeled that and cubed it up. When I judged the meat was tendered through, I put the potato pieces in. I likewise sliced an onion into the pan. Finally I opened the can of green beans I'd bought at Eula Jarboe's store in Wolver and stirred those into the mess. I saw that, preacher or no preacher, Simon had a bottle of red wine on his shelf to cook with and I added some of that. While I

waited for it all to stew together, I picked my guitar and sang some of the "Tree Beside the Waters" hymn:

> I'll pitch my tent on this campground,
> Old Satan ain't about to fling me down . . .

Simon walked in right then, a-carrying a big hobby of green cedar, a stack that high above him he sort of swayed under it. "I've always liked that song, John," he said.

Here's how he made me a mattress on the floor by the fireplace. He put a close-set row of tips, then he laid another on top with the leaves over the first and the butts to the floor; then more on those, like courses of shingles. He put them down so thick and careful that they made a layer near about a foot thick. By the time he'd finished, so was my stew ready. We dished it out on two plates, and it made supper enough for both of us.

Simon praised it to the high heavens. He did more; he poured us glasses of wine from the bottle, and allowed that there's something in favor of wine in the Book of Proverbs. He got down his Bible to prove it.

" 'Give strong drink unto him that is ready to perish, and wine unto those that be of heavy hearts,' " he read out the verse to me. " 'Let him drink, and forget his poverty, and remember his misery no more.' "

"I do hope and pray neither one of us is ready to perish right yet," I said, and had a good sip from my glass. "Though I can be sure enough heavyhearted about Wolver, and the misery those folks make themselves suffer from."

"You talk like a merciful man, John, and your being here lightens my own heart, for I've been lonely now and then in this little cabin. I keep telling myself that you've been sent here to drive out the evil."

Naturally, he couldn't know how close to the truth he was; though he thought of the sending of me as from another place than Washington, and by another higher authority than Washington. I still didn't explain it to him.

Instead, I got him to talk more things about witchcraft in general and Wolver in particular, such ground as we'd started to go over before. Things like about what a coven is and how, from the way things looked, there purely had to be more than one coven in Wolver itself, what with all the folks caught up in the belief. And how several covens would join together under a bigger chief, and how in Wolver, that was bound to be Tiphaine. Simon no more than guessed about her, like the man I'd talked to at the Trail Motel. He hadn't air seen her, but he figured she was the biggest of the bunch in power and evil, and all the others jumped to obey her slightest word of bidding.

"Whatever beats me is, they worship at that old church," I said. "That's more than I can figure. You'd reckon that they'd stay out of a churchyard, of all places."

"Not them," said Simon. "They love an old deserted church, where once there was a preacher to say the gospel word, where now the preacher and the people have gone away—deserted it. They love to come and mock it and dirty it. That's the big thing for them to do, mock and sort of rebel against churches. I've heard tell that they go out at night through church burying grounds and dig up bodies and cut off their fingers and toes to use in charms."

I hiked my shoulders to keep the shudder out of them. "I'd call that the lowest of all things to do."

"Near about the lowest, even for that range of folks."

When we got through with eating our supper, we had us another glass of wine each, and Simon pushed the cork back into the bottle. Then we washed the dishes. It was close to dark by then, and Simon lighted up his old oil lamp and fetched it from the fireboard to the table. I spread out my blankets on that evergreen mattress. We sat down and talked for a spell, about what those low-down, crazy-headed people in Wolver might could possibly be up to a-doing.

"All this devil-worship business makes me wonder myself about something," I said finally. "Is there a sure-enough Satan? Who knows so much?"

"I'd make a guess that there's a whole sight more people believe in Satan than believe in any sort of god," said Simon. "Anyway, if there isn't a Satan, there's something working almighty hard to pretend to be one. You can judge that from all the devilish things that go on in this world. And there's now and then somebody who's got to make it his job to fight against those things." He slitted his wise eyes at me. "That's what I've thought more than once or twice about you. That you're somebody who's come here to fight against them, sort of like old Matthew Hopkins."

Again, I had to keep from a-speaking the whole truth. "Matthew Hopkins," I repeated him. "I've read a few things about how he did in old England, and I've heard talk. They can't count up how many folks he did to death for witchcraft, killed them in the name of the king, and a right many of them were innocent."

"I didn't mean you were like Hopkins in character. Maybe some way in duty."

It was high time to change the subject. "Simon, I keep on a-wondering myself how it comes that the sun doesn't shine clear in the sky over this part of the country."

"And I've told you, I don't know how to answer that. What I said was, that sort of weather thing set in about the time the devil crowd took charge in Wolver."

It was my turn to look at him hard. "What you have in mind is that they cause it, for some reason or other."

"Sometimes I think it's probably that," he said, "but what their reason might be, that's beyond me to know."

"Did you ever try aught to clear the sky?"

"No," he said, and he shook his head. "That's beyond me,

too. But we're getting nowhere with all this wondering and supposing. Let's relax a little. How about playing your guitar, John? Not necessarily hymns this time."

I took that for a good idea, and I didn't give him an argument about it. What I picked and sang was a bunch of country songs like "I Hope Tomorrow Never Comes" and "Fire in the Mountains" and "Lily of Arkansas." Simon purely relished to hear me do that. He patted his hands to keep time for the music, and once he even got up and did a few steps of a buck dance, right spry. "I learned to do that before ever I got my call to preach," he said, grinning.

It grew late of the night with us a-doing that. Finally Simon blew out his lamp and we lay down, he on his cot bed, while I stretched out on my evergreen mattress. I, at least, went right off to sleep, there on those good-smelling cedar branches. I did have me a dream about something or other. I thought I was a-making my way through thorn bushes, with the thorns a-sticking into me on both sides, but in the dream I got out the other end all right. That dream, allows the old belief, means you'll win out in a rough, scary situation. And it was plumb good to hope that that was the truth.

The blur-faced sun came up and shone in at the window and woke us both. I put on clean socks and shirt when I dressed. Simon cooked us some oatmeal, and we had that with sugar and canned milk and mugs of black coffee. When the dishes were done, I filled a tin basin and washed myself up good. I got out my razor and shaved a couple days of beard off my face. Then I wet my thick, dark hair and combed it to make it look the best I possibly could.

"All right," I said, "I'm a-going for a walk into town."

"Town?" Simon repeated me, and frowned up his face.

"Into Wolver."

"No, sir." He put up a hand at me, like a traffic policeman. "Nothing doing. Why, that would be the worst possible thing you could do."

"It would be the best possible thing I could do." It was hard to say something sensible, without a-telling what I'd promised the man at the Trail Motel. "They likely figure they'd hammered me helpless in that fight, or either if I'd got to where I could move, I'd turned and run off for fear. But I'm a-going to show myself to them, show them there's naught they can do to run me off."

Simon scowled deeper yet. "I'd better come along with you."

"No," I said in my turn, stubborn as a yellow mule. "I'm a-going in there alone. So you just wait round here for me."

He didn't like that air bit, but he saw that I'd made my mind up to it. I put on my wide old hat—somehow or other I hadn't lost it in all my troubles—and left the house and walked out to the rutted road and pointed myself toward Wolver.

It seemed a well-worn, well-known way to me by now. Even the gravel of it that scrunched under my boots felt familiar. I made it round the bend betwixt the thickets of trees, and saw the place where I'd gone in to make my camp the first night. The cloaked sun overhead made the morning hot, it baked the road I walked on.

Past that camping place, I slogged along past the old church. I felt sorry all over again for its ruin and what had come to it after it got ruined. Simon had said that all the praying and Bible reading in the old days couldn't save it from Tiphaine and her everlasting devil crowd; it would just urge them on. Things had been another sight safer in Simon's little cabin with his hawthorn bushes and horseshoe, in reach of the eye from the smoke from his Beltane fires. I agreed myself that he had more or less the right of it not to overlook air bet in the fight against evil.

Once quit of the church, I'd tramped into sight of the settlement. There were those houses on both sides of the

road as I came in. And in the different yards, folks on the
move round, like ants round their hills.

I reached the first place on whatever Wolver might could
call its main street. By that time, I knew that cabin-built
house, with the fence in front and, at its back, a washing of
clothes hung up on a line. At least, they kept clean in that
house if they washed clothes; but to me the clothes looked
crazy-made, not what I'd expect human men and women and
children to wear. They were all crumpled and sneaky as they
hung on the line. They looked—well, call them evil. Not like
honest clothes.

In the front yard were some of those Wolver children I'd
seen before. A little small girl with an apron on, and two
shirttail boys—no pants that I could make out, just long shirts
down to their bare feet. They saw me, too, with their big dull
eyes in their skinny faces, under hair that trailed down on
their foreheads, like the sprawly legs of a hundred spiders. I
stopped in front of their fence and flung up a hand to them.

"Hey, you all," I hailed them. "What kind of day you all
a-having for yourselves?"

They looked on me with their goggle eyes. They might
could have been so many little wild animals.

"What you all up to this morning?" I inquired them.

"It's John yonder!" squeaked out one, in a voice like a bat
at night. And all the three of them came sort of a-stumbling
forward, toward the fence where I stood.

"You youngins get back here!" shrilled a woman from the
front door of the house, and all three children pulled back
again. The woman looked out on me, with a frightened stare
on her fat face. You'd have thought I was a hungry wild wolf
or the like. It might could have been that's how I seemed to
her, right then.

So I walked along the street from where they feared me
thattaway.

Another house and fenced yard next to that one. A long, scroungy-looking man was out a-sitting on his doorlog, at work to fit a new handle into an old ax head. He looked to be a-having his troubles with it. He whittled at the wood, tried the head to see would it fit, then whittled some more.

When he looked up and saw me a-using along outside his fence, he jumped up the way you'd think somebody had stuck a pitchfork into him. I saw his face as he lifted it, and there was a big, puffy black place under the eye. I wondered myself if maybe he was one of the bunch that had ganged up on me a couple of nights ago on the road past the church. "Hey," I called out to him, but he slid back into his house like a lizard.

These folks didn't have aught of use for me, I guessed, didn't relish to get close to me. I studied if that could be because I was maybe supposed to be dead, or scared out of Wolver, or some way both the two. I studied about a-getting somebody to talk to me, and thought of Ottom Orcutt.

Yonder ahead was his forge, and he was in it. His hammer went clank, clank on hot iron. I turned thattaway to walk in on him.

"Oh," from behind me said a deep, rich voice I'd learned to know. "Welcome back, John. Welcome back to Wolver."

I swung round to look. There at the gateway across the street stood Tiphaine. She wore another dress this time, light blue that shone like a polished sapphire. It was cut low and came down off her creamy shoulders. It fitted her proud body like as if it had been varnished onto her.

"Well I knew you'd come again," she called across to me.

Ottom had stopped his pounding to look, too. Gentlemen, she was worth a man's time to look at her. I walked over toward her, right up to her gate. She watched me air step of the way.

"I'm truly glad you're not hurt, after all," she said, a-making it sound like as if she sure enough meant that thing. "My friends—well, they rather lost their heads. If they hurt you, it wasn't by my wish, my order. I've been somewhat harsh to the ones who attacked you."

"You said just now that you knew I'd be back," I reminded her. "What does that mean, how came you to know that?"

"I made a call to you," she replied me, with a smile that was downright glorious. "At sunrise, I spoke your name in a certain fashion. And here you are."

Sure enough, there I was. I'd told the government man I'd do it. I'd told Simon I'd do it. But how much of it was some sort of doing by Tiphaine?

She moved back from the gate. "Come in, John," she invited me, still with her smile. "You and I have so much to say to each other."

CHAPTER 11

In through the gateway I came. I recollect that my feet felt right numb, though the day sure enough wasn't cold.

"I made a call to you," Tiphaine said again, and I vow her voice petted me, like a hand laid on me. "I called in my heart, and so you came."

"No, Tiphaine," I said to her. "I came here on my own hook. I reckoned I'd just as well show you all that I wasn't hurt or either scared out, night before last."

"But you've come, and that's the truly important thing. Now that you're here, let's go into the house."

Together we walked, side by side, along the stone flags to her porch. In spite of what I'd said about my own hook, it was someway like as if I couldn't choose but come along with her at her bidding. Somebody's feet sounded behind us, and quick I looked back.

"Don't be nervous, that's only Ottom," Tiphaine said. "I beckoned him to follow us. He'll be profited by what you and I find worth deciding together."

As we headed for the door, it opened to us. Quill Norbury was there, all rough-dressed-up this time, in a blue-checked old shirt and brown pants with a patch on one knee. You'd have reckoned he'd come to wash the windows.

"Good morning, John," he said, like the host man at a party, but his face seemed to wonder itself at me. Tiphaine and I went into the hall, with Ottom a-tramping close behind us. He only looked on me, nair word did he speak. His mouth showed cut and raw and swollen. I'd done that to him the first time we met, and likely I'd added a little bit onto it, out on the road when his bunch ganged up on me.

Inside, by the dark Earth Mother statue, stood two others, and the statue's eyes seemed to shine and watch me. "John, let me introduce our friend Burroughs," said Tiphaine, a-talking like a nice lady at a friendly get-together.

"Hey," he said. He was the tallowy fellow who'd made war talk with me the first quarter hour I was in Wolver. He was marked, too, a knuckle gash on his left cheek. My knuckle gash.

"And here," Tiphaine gestured her hand. "We call him Gaufridi."

He nodded me without air, word. He was a dry, grayish man who might could have been in his thirties or fifties, or air year in betwixt those ages.

"Burroughs," I repeated Tiphaine. "Gaufridi. Seems like to me, I've heard tell those names before now."

"They're simple, convenient *noms de guerre*, though we don't intend to wage war on you." She smiled her sweet friendliest. "Burroughs was once the name of a highly interesting divine in old Salem up in Massachusetts. Much to his discomfiture, he was hanged one day in August of sixteen ninety-two, if I remember the date rightly. And the name Gaufridi recalls another ecclesiastic, a truly charming man who flourished in southern France *circa* sixteen ten and who also had a most untimely and unlucky death. These neighbors of ours have chosen to adopt those distinguished new designations."

Which, I reminded myself, fitted right in with what the government man had talked about; how somebody a-joining in with a witch crowd took him a new name for the new work he'd chosen to do.

"And now, gentlemen," said Tiphaine to the four of them, "John and I are going to have a little private conference, there in the sitting room. I'll ask you others to wait here, just in case I want you later."

"But of course, Tiphaine," said Norbury, which as I reckoned was all he could say when she talked thattaway to him. He quartered me over with his eye, the way a man would do who wanted to be dead certain sure how air square inch of me looked.

"Then, if you will, John."

Together she and I went to the open inner door, and into her sitting room. She shut the door behind us, and I heard the snick of its shutting.

"Alone together, John," she said and smiled at me, and almost nudged against me with her bare white shoulder. "Shall we sit down together as we did before?"

I'd been in that room twice already, and it was by and large the way I recollected it, with its hanging curtains and the figures on them, the chairs, the shiny-topped table. Tiphaine pulled back a chair to sit down, and so did I. She put her hand on the wine jug that was there.

"And will you have a drink with me again, John?" she invited me, a-leaning at me with her smile. "But wait a moment, this time you won't have to change cups. I'll prove your cup for you. Watch this."

She filled a silver cup and put it to her red, red lips and drank. "There," she said, and she shoved it across the table to me. "I wouldn't have poisoned myself, would I? Not without good cause, naturally. But what is it that seems to interest you?"

"This doll-baby thing here," I said.

It lay at the exact middle of the tabletop, a little man-figure of a thing, round about a foot long. Tiphaine poured wine into another cup for herself.

"Do you recognize the likeness, perhaps?" she asked.

When she inquired me that thing, I did me a study of the

figure. It was made out of wax, as I could see, and it was shaped long and lathy, and it wore what looked to be work clothes like mine, and a little broad-brimmed hat like mine. Its hair, what of it bushed into sight below the hat, must have been made of bunches of soft, dark thread. Its pink-painted face had a good length of nose like mine, and two eyes made out of black, shiny beads. It lay on its back with its arms and legs flung out.

"Why," I said at last, "whosoever made that thing was right clever with the hands."

"Thank you, John. It was I who made it, the best I could. Very well, and what do you think of those objects beside it? Observe them, but I'd advise you against touching them."

I bent to the table to take a close look at what she mentioned. They were two little small stone arrowheads, one of pink flint, the other of white. They were right prettily made, in the shape of the slim leaves of a weeping willow, and they were no longer than the first two joints of a man's finger. They were flaked to sharp, lean points.

"I'd reckon that Indians made those," I said. "I've seen the like before this, one place another, turned up by plowshares. The Indians were right clever at that stone-chipping."

She shook her head, and her black hair swept from one bare shoulder to the other.

"No, John, not Indians. Those are elf arrows. I've sometimes asked myself if the elves, or whatever creatures we call elves, first taught the Indians how to make such things. But these came from abroad—from England—and their particular powers have been proved, over and over again. What do you suppose would happen if one or both of them were stabbed into this interesting little likeness of you?"

I took in a long breath. "Why, all I can say as to that," I replied her, "all I can say is, try it and see."

She shone her green eyes. "Wouldn't you be afraid if I did?"

"No, Tiphaine, I'd not be afraid one shuck. In this hard life I've lived, I got over a-being afraid a long while back."

"How admirable of you, but isn't fear the beginning of wisdom?"

"They say the fear of the Lord is."

She watched me a second or two or three. "You're not drinking." Cheerful-faced again, she took her cup in her hand. "Come now, let's drink to a better and more profitable acquaintance."

She drank, and I drank with her, and sure enough I relished that good wine. I waited for her to come out with what it was she seemed to hope for from me.

"It so happens that I know something more about you than when you first appeared so dramatically in Wolver the other day," she said then. "Within an hour of when you came, I sent out an inquiry for more information on the interesting subject of you."

"You flatter me," I said. "I never did reckon that I counted that much with you."

"But you do, and shall I tell you what the information is that has come back to me? John, you've been a problem here and there. In your wanderings, you've worked some fairly unpleasant effects against people like my friends and me."

"Your friends and you," I repeated her.

"My friends are all those who plead for truth and aren't too frequently heard. You've hindered them—people like, say, Mr. Onselm and Mr. Howsen and Shull Cobart. You've put obstacles in the way of the work we try to do, John. But I think that's because you didn't know better."

"I've tried to do two–three things in this world," I said, "and I've always tried to do them right, the best I can. I always will."

She looked away from me and studied that wax image on the table. Then: "You must realize that I've been more than merciful to you. For instance, I haven't tried anything lethal on this poppet, nothing that would hurt you. And why? Because I still have some hopes of convincing you as to what's the right thing to do."

"I've spent my own life a-trying to do right things."

"And what are the right things?" she asked me, and played with her empty silver cup. "Just how do you define right and wrong? For instance, do you think that our worship here is wrong? Tell me, John, what's the verdict of the law of our land on the worship and science we practice?"

"I know how to answer that," I replied her, a-recollecting my talk with the government man at the county seat. "All worship is free, no matter what."

"True," she said, and nodded. "There's no law against any sort of worship. And there never was, on the statute books of any state since this country was founded. The old English laws, the ones in force, the ones enforced when things happened so sadly in Salem, never got into the books when America's founders made their own books. All you can find today are statutes and ordinances against false claims of divination—only liars and poseurs need tremble at those. Not honest worshippers."

"Why, sure," I said, my eyes back on what she called the poppet. When she had worked out the face on it, she had known right well what I looked like. Only I was some browner in the skin than the pink that was painted on.

"You've been a sore danger to certain curious creatures and casters of spells and wise men and women, for what motives I won't exactly assign just now. You've a considerable reputation for that. But perhaps you're only more or less a busybody. At least, I haven't heard of any great profit you've gained from those efforts."

"No, not if you're a-talking about money or like that, Tiphaine," I agreed her. "I've not much sought for money. But, a-speaking about profit, I wonder myself about you."

"Well, now." And she smiled. "I'm a mystery to you. That's intriguing."

"I'm not even dead sure that your name is Tiphaine."

That took the smile right off her face. Her green eyes glittered at me. From somewhere, maybe in her lap, she'd fetched out a rod of shiny black wood. It was more or less a foot and a half long, and its two tips were hard white, like ivory. She fiddled with it in her jeweled hands.

"Tiphaine is my name," she said between her white teeth. "I chose it for myself. That's enough for you. Or is it? Tell me more about what you find mysterious about me."

"Well," I said. "I study over in my mind why you live in this little settlement, off away from the rest of the world. What's in it for you, here in Wolver? Who do you work for at whatever it is you work at? And, when it comes to profits, what's the profit to you?"

"Those are good questions," she said, a-putting the rod on the table next to the little wax image. "I hope you're having fun as you try to come up with the answers."

"It shouldn't much surprise you to hear I think you're a beautiful woman," I said to her. "As beautiful as a man could hope to meet up with in long miles. And I figure you for smart and gifted in a heap of ways. What might could you be a-doing for yourself out in the big world, with those things?"

She frowned over that. It might could have made her a little mad.

"Then what would you suggest, John? Should I become an actress on the stage or in moving pictures? I've been asked to do that in my time. Or marrying some rich man with all his pockets full of money? I've been asked to do that, too—often. To live in some stylish place, go to women's clubs, preside over big dinners?" Her black mane of hair rustled as she shook it at me. "There are many sorts of profits, John. You must have found out for yourself that you don't gain a profit of one sort without giving up profit of another sort. Quite a few philosophers agree on that point. And that's quite enough for you about my possible wishes and motives."

"Yes, ma'am," I said, as quiet as I could make the words. "It should ought to be enough for you, too, when you reckon on my possible wishes and motives."

"*Touché*," she cried out, cheerful again. "Isn't this a beginning of a friendly understanding between us? You have a good mind, yourself. Why not open it and consider the question of what may be right, after all?"

"You mean, the worship of devils," I suggested.

"Worship of the oldest and mightiest of all spirits. You heard me a little on the subject, night before last." She leaned herself across the table at me, with her green eyes and black hair and white shoulders. "Think of so many great men charged with ill magic, when they only wanted to increase human knowledge, increase service to the world."

Now she pleaded to me, begged to me.

"Magic and supernatural wisdom have been mankind's strength and salvation since the beginning of the human race," she said. "They have been mocked and persecuted, but they're justified, they're right and enlightened. In their teachings is necessary progress for all peoples, everywhere."

"You remarked such things here the other night," I said, a-watching her.

"More wine, John, now that you know it's not drugged or poisoned?"

"No, I thank you, I've had a plenty."

She poured into her own cup, and drank. "Hear what I say. Every brilliant thinker, every bringer of new truths, has been misunderstood and persecuted by workaday religionists, by dull, conservative, jealous rulers." She gestured. "Roger Bacon was the wisest and best man of his century, and when he declared great scientific truths, he was imprisoned as a

black magician. Joan of Arc saved France, and was burnt at
the stake for a witch. Galileo was disciplined for daring to say
that the earth moves around the sun, and was threatened and
browbeaten into taking it back. Paracelsus, who would have
given great medical advances to suffering people, was reviled
and accused. If Freud and Einstein had lived three hundred
years ago, they'd have met the same dangers."

Her voice didn't purr when she said those things, it rang
out like a bugle. If she'd been a lawyer, a-pleading a case in
court, the judge and jury would have hung onto air word she
spoke. I took down the last sip of wine in my cup.

"Those folks you name weren't sure-enough magic people,"
I said. "They didn't hold with magic. They were just smarter
than most, and, I agree you, if you're that smart you can get
yourself into trouble now and then."

"You're able to see things accurately, John, see hidden
truth. For how many years, then, has truth been martyred, ex-
communicated, abused? You seem to recognize those classic
names I spoke. You're wise, informed. You must have read
some interesting books."

"Yes, ma'am, now and then I've looked me into a good
few, and I've always done my best to hark at wise folks and
learn things to think about."

"But yet," she said, "you're not truly aware of what poten-
tial you have. From what I've learned about you, you've been
a wanderer—a tramp, some would say—and you've fought and
won fights. But always you've been like a child playing with
tools and weapons he doesn't understand. Understanding:
That's the key word. With instruction, you can be great
among us. I've already foretold you that."

"Great amongst you," I repeated her. "What kind of
great?"

"Why, as possessor of wisdom and the power that goes
with it. As chief of our Grand Sabbat."

"Sabbat? Wasn't that what I stumbled onto at the church grounds? I hate to say it, but I wasn't air great much impressed."

"That was a minor event," she said. "We observe it every few weeks. But the Grand Sabbat happens only once in seven years. Seven—the lucky number."

"Seven days of the week," I nodded her. "Seven holy angels."

"Seven, the winning number on a throw of the dice," she said. "Seven spirits of dread night power in ancient Assyria; seven ocean seas; seven continents, of which the newest to be discovered and the one most full of mystery is Antarctica. Our seventh year at Wolver draws to its end. Indeed, we count it as completed in three days and three nights from now."

"Three," I said after her. "That's another lucky number."

"Pythagoras called three the perfect number, with a beginning, a middle and an end. Three days until our Grand Sabbat. Those three days will be enough to make you ready to preside."

"What would I do if I presided?"

"You'd be bowed down to, worshipped by the whole Sabbat. Your slightest order would be absolute law. You would clasp and claim the queen of the Grand Sabbat."

"I see," said I. "And you'd be the queen."

"Naturally," she said, smiling. "Extremely naturally. Love is a prize factor at the Grand Sabbat. You've surmised that, I'm sure."

And I'd swear, she wiggled herself at me as she said that thing, like some flirty young girl at a play party. Oh, she was a-making a set at me, and no I reckon about it.

"This Grand Sabbat will see us joined and upheld by distinguished adepts from other communities. From other nations, even." She sounded like somebody who knew what she was a-talking about. "There are certain governments that approve and support us abroad. They are sending representatives."

I could have told her how I'd heard tell something about that already, but I didn't. "Governments," I said after her. "I've always heard it said that your crowd is against governments."

"When it is our right and fate to rule, we'll be our own government. When the whole world is ready to recognize and accept our wisdom. And that day will come soon."

Now she was a-talking like somebody who says a piece committed to memory. I reckoned to myself that she must have repeated all those things before this, to convince somebody else. But it was something to hear, gentlemen, and she was something to see. She leaned herself forward on the table and reached out her slim hand to put on top of mine.

"You're listening, John. You're convinced. You'll be one of us."

"One of you?"

"One of the very foremost among us. You'll command, and be obeyed. You'll have power of life and death—"

"No," I said, and took my hand away from under hers and stood up.

"What are you saying?" She was on her feet, too. "I said, command—power—"

"And I said no," I cut in on her, and grinned. "I don't want to have power over air living soul, and I don't want air living soul to have power over me. No part of such a thing, thank you kindly." I turned round. "Good-bye, Tiphaine, I'll be a-going."

"No, you won't be going. Not after you heard all that I said."

She slapped her hands together, so sharp it sounded like a pistol shot. In came those four men from out in the hall.

"I've just told John that he won't be going," she said to them. "He'll stay right here until he comes to his senses."

They made themselves into a line and started toward me, a slow six inches at a time. I stood myself easy, hands at my side, half-fisted. I picked up Ottom's eyes with mine.

"Seems to me like as if you're a slow learner," I joshed him. "Twice now, you and I have tangled, and twice I've slapped you down. Third time will be the charm."

"We'll see about that," Tiphaine downright screeched from where she stood beside the table.

She'd picked up her black rod, and now she touched one ivory tip of it to the figure of me there before her.

Right that same moment, I felt like as if all the strength had run out of me like water. I swayed back and forth on my feet, I near about dropped over. But not quite.

"Take hold of him," ordered Tiphaine, her rod still held to that figure on the table.

Ottom and the fat one they called Burroughs stepped in and grabbed me by the arms. They near about had to hold me up on my feet. I'd gone plumb weak, I was blood-drained. But I could still see and hear, I could still feel. She hadn't captured that away from me.

"Get him yonder into the little room," Tiphaine commanded them, her voice the fiercest I'd yet heard it. "You know the room I mean, Quill. I'll hold this to his image, I'll keep him helpless until he's safely shut up."

At that, I tried to shake free, but I was puny as water. They clamped onto me. I heard Ottom say a swear word in my ear.

"Keep him tight," said Tiphaine, "but don't hurt him. Not yet. We're by no means through with our friend John."

Quill Norbury had quick trotted to the red curtains at the back of the room, and he pulled on a cord that made them slide open to right and left. I saw a stone wall, as gray-green as dirty water that's been frozen into chunks. Midway along showed a narrow door that looked to be made up of black iron plates. In the upper half of the door was set a little window with shiny brass bars, and below that, a brass lock as big as a sardine can. Quill turned a key with a loud, wrenchy sound and dragged the door open.

Ottom and the Burroughs fellow dragged me along to it. They shoved me through into a room beyond. It was dark in there, but I was able to make out a chair. I sat myself down, weak as a baby child. Quill Norbury followed me in and put a silver-looking bowl on a little square table at the middle of the floor. A sort of glow soaked out of the bowl, like some kind of pale fire.

"I'd advise you not to touch that ember, John," Tiphaine's voice called to me from the big room. "Not unless you want to hurry things along to your end."

Quill trotted out and shut the door. I heard the lock scrape, to keep me in. In the next second, my strength came back to me, all through air muscle.

I reckoned that meant that Tiphaine had taken the rod away from the image of me. Up I jumped and quick ran to the door. I grabbed the heavy brass bars of the peephole and dragged on them, the hardest I could.

The door didn't even budge, didn't even creak.

CHAPTER 12

All right, John, I allowed to myself, now's a good time to see where it is they've shoved you away.

The sound of that heavy iron lock a-turning in the door was how I'd always reckoned it would sound to be flung under the jail; though I'd nair been in a jail, had just visited two–three of them in my time, a-trying to get somebody out who didn't belong to be in there. Well, I reckoned, there I was. Tiphaine, her own law and gospel in Wolver, had done made a prisoner out of me.

The sharp, pale light from the silver bowl on the table was a plenty to see by. I could make out the whole room. It was more or less fifteen feet by ten, as I guessed it then and figured it later by a-stepping off the length and width of the floor. I moved thissaway and that in it. The walls had a sort of soft, pale blue color to them, almost like skimmed milk. When I put my finger up against one, it felt as slick as a china plate. Likely this was some kind of enamel, on plaster that seemed to be laid over heavy stones. The wall didn't echo when I gave it a thump with my fist.

There was furniture in there. The table with the bowl of light, and beside the bowl a big, shadowy-covered book. A heavy-made wooden chair with a bottom woven of strips of juniper bark. At the far corner of the room, a sort of sofa bed, made up with blankets so dark-colored they looked next to about black. No carpet on the tiled floor, that was a purply red shade, like spoiled plums. Beyond the cot, a door made of one pale, enameled plank. I walked across to that and opened it. The pale light reached in and showed me that it was a little small bathroom in there, shower and basin and toilet, all of them clean as clean. That was the whole of the picture of where I'd been locked up.

On the long wall across from the locked door hung a piece of what looked to be the same cloth as those dark blankets on the bed. I shoved it aside, and daylight flowed in. I saw a little window with the murky glow of the sun out yonder, amongst trees and flowery bushes, their leaves a-standing up like listening ears. Haze lay there in the branches. The window likewise had heavy up-and-down brass bars, set as stoutly into the plastered sills above and below as if they'd been rooted in there like the stems of trees. Even before I laid my hold on them and tried to shake them, I well knew there'd be no chance of getting out thattaway.

I took me a few seconds to study what was outside the window. It was thickety, and the flowers had their strange look, like as if eyes were set in them to look in at me through the little window. One tree hung right close to the house, with droopy branches to it like a weeping willow, though that wasn't the kind of tree it was. Amongst its hanging branches there was a stir and ripple, but whatever that was, it couldn't be a bird. I'd found out that birds didn't sing or fly or yet stir branches round Wolver.

All right, folks used to name it that if you got in somewhere you could get out again. I'd better study the whole place over, up and down, into air corner of it.

I did that thing. I stepped back from the window and tapped the walls, tapped them again, and they sounded as solid as the rock face in a quarry. Naught to say there was a hidden panel somewhere. I stomped back and forth across the floor, and it sounded just as solid. I got up and stood on the chair and tapped the ceiling and tapped it, one place after another. I could just as well have tapped the floor. Into the bathroom I looked, I went over it with eyes and fingers. Unless I could yank out a pipe and make myself little enough to slide out the hole, naught to do there. As for the door to the big room, it was built of iron plates it would need an acetylene torch to knock apart. I did find there was a closed slot, not big enough to stick your arm through, with a trap to fit over it outside. If I was to get out, then, it would have to be that door.

Finally I took myself back and sat down in the chair, as easy as I could make myself. "Bravo, John," said Tiphaine's musical voice through the barred hole in the door, and I could hear her hands a-patting together, like the applause at a show. "You're acting the part of a true philosopher.

"Don't you find it rather quiet and boresome in there?" she inquired me, with a laugh somewhere in her voice. "Wouldn't it be more pleasant to be out here with me, all alone here with me?"

"If you're all alone out yonder," I said back to her, "you know another sight better than to let me out with you."

Her mouth made a sort of red O. "Do you mean you'd treat me violently? You'd be so ungallant as to do that? Then, yes, you're better off in there, behind these stout bars. You can, perhaps, make up your mind to a more reasonable outlook on things. That is, if you hope to come out alive."

"I reckon that means you figure to kill me in here."

"Once before, and very sadly, I told you that that could happen. And that your body would never be found."

"I give you a week," I said, "and friends of mine would be here in Wolver to find my body, and they'd be right unpleasant about it."

She laughed, like sweet, soft music. "Friends of yours will come to find your body? Then, on second thought, perhaps I'll let them find it, then join them in mourning your untimely death from a stoppage of the heart. How sad for you, but how dolefully a natural cause for the end of a man's life. Any medical examination would show simple stoppage of your heart."

"There's naught wrong with my heart," I said. "There nair was."

"Not so far in your adventurous career, John," she said, and that smile thinned out on her face. "You declared, if I remember rightly, that you'd give me a week. I'm forced to be less generous than that with you. I can give you only three days. Those three days I spoke of before."

"Up until your Great Sabbat, or Grand Sabbat, or whatever it is you call it?"

"You can be at that meeting, John, happy among us. Or, if you're stubborn, you can stay here."

"Then I'll stay here," I said.

"If you do that, you'll come to wish you hadn't. Just before you stop wishing anything, knowing anything." She smiled and shone her eyes on me. "Excuse me now."

She moved off away, out of my sight through the bars. I heard her go to the outer door to the big room. Then I tried to shove my hand through the bars, see if I might could reach to the big key in the lock. But I couldn't get my hand out more than past the wrist. So I went back and sat in the chair and tried my best to think things out.

I wondered myself if I'd been a fool just to tell Tiphaine a flat "hell, no" thattaway, if I'd not maybe have done it better to make off like as if I went along with her notions. If I'd done that when we talked before, instead of a-getting up to walk out on her and not a-making it. I wondered myself that, and couldn't rightly reply myself on it.

I sat my easiest, and thought over how once I'd talked to a fellow who'd been years in state prison. How he'd said, "When they lock you up in there, all you got to do is remember." So I remembered.

First off, I thought on myself as a little young boy in the Drowning Creek country, my father and mother dead in their graves before I scarcely knew them and a good-hearted schoolteacher took me in to raise. How she'd taught me to read and write, and how I'd more or less taught myself to pick the guitar. How an old man I'd known gave me silver strings to put on my guitar, how they'd seemed like as if they had their own strength and knowledge of things. How I'd grown up and gone to one of the senseless wars this crazy-headed world keeps on a-bringing on itself, what it had been like to fight for your life and be grateful for not a-getting killed. How I'd roamed these mountains, how I'd joined in to do big sings and been clapped and cheered by those who harked at me. And beautiful women who'd leaned to me like kittens to a bowl of milk, and how of them all I loved only the one, a girl called Evadare. And the dangers I'd found and faced up to, some of which I've told you all about and some I don't care much even to think on air time, and how I'd come safe through them all so far; though sometimes it was just the thickness of a hair betwixt me and whatair end comes to life. All the way I went over those remembries, right up to when the United States government gave me the word from the President his own self to come to Wolver and see what was what.

So I'd come to Wolver, and here I was in Wolver, in Tiphaine's house, under lock and key. When I looked back on it, I reckoned I'd been in danger practically air step I'd taken here and yonder. Danger had been my breakfast, dinner and supper.

I could think someway about what was to happen. Tiphaine had done something to me by touching her wand to that wax image of me, and when she'd had me safe behind a lock she'd taken the wand away. Three days was what she'd said she gave me. She had hopes of me still, big hopes of some kind, and during those three days she'd try to make them come true.

What were those hopes?

Well, these torn-down Wolver folks wanted me to join up with them. I'd heard a right big bunch of promises made if I'd join. And likewise, that last promise Tiphaine had made about what would happen to me if I didn't join.

If I held out, I'd have a last moment to wish I'd done what I was bid, before I was all through a-wishing and a-fighting and a-living. That's what her mocking words meant. I reckoned that she was so used to a-getting her way in all things, it pestered her to have me hold off and refuse to kneel before her magic powers.

Something that once had happened came into my mind, and I laughed. Just a quiet, short laugh, but a laugh came back to me through the barred hole in the door.

"The situation seems to amuse you, John," said Tiphaine, from where she'd come back to spy on me again.

"That's right," I said. "I laughed some."

"Tell me what it is that you laughed at, and perhaps we can laugh together. That's always a comfortable situation, laughter shared between two."

I looked round where I sat, without a-getting up. "Maybe the thing wasn't so funny, at that," I said. "After all, a man died when it happened."

"Yet if we laughed more at death, we might be less afraid of death." She sounded downright like some happy friend. "Go on, John, tell me about it. It will help pass the time."

"You gave me three days before something happened to me," I said. "This other thing, it was when I was given thirteen."

She drew in her breath long. I could see her face, her shining hair, through the bars in the door hole. "Thirteen," she said, "the number of a coven."

I'd heard tell a right much about covens, as I've already said, but I nair remarked on it then. "This thing happened to me with a fellow named Joss Kift. He was a witch-spell man, he conjured and all like that. He had a lot of folks purely scared."

"Joss Kift," she said the name after me. "I think I've heard of him. But there are so many names, I can't charge my memory with all of them."

"You asked me to tell you the tale. All right, so Joss Kift was right mad with me because I'd allowed that all his witch-talk was nothing but lies. He told me, with others a-harking, that I'd die in thirteen unlucky days."

"But apparently you didn't," Tiphaine said.

"No, ma'am, I'm here, I nair died that time. Those thirteen days passed one by one, with each day a something a-happening to scare me. Once I found a doll made to look like me, and stuck in where its heart would ought to be was a big black pin." I stopped a second, to think of the image of me she'd made. "Then a black rooster with its head cut off, a-lying in the path I was a-going on. And another time, a black dog, a-hanging dead by its neck, to a tree branch."

"Joss Kift, you called him? He seems to have had some science. I'd like to talk to him."

"I'm sorry, but you can't talk to him now. He's past the talking to. All right, the thirteenth day passed, and the thirteenth night came, and it was a right stormy one. I was laid out on a pallet that had been made up for me in Tram Colley's cabin, and my friends all round it tried to get me to move, sit up, talk to them. Outside in that black, stormy night, we heard a stick a-breaking up, and then again and again. Thirteen breaks to it. They popped sharp."

"I see," she said. "And then?"

"Why, then, Joss Kift popped his head in through the window to laugh down at me. When I sat up and grabbed onto him, he just dropped over on the sill. He died, right then and there. When the sheriff and the county coroner got there, they allowed he'd been struck by that same thing you said. Stoppage of the heart."

I crossed one leg over my other knee and sat the easiest I could in the chair.

Then's when Tiphaine laughed herself, a laugh like a silver bell rung to signal something you don't want to happen to you.

"A fascinating story, and I believe it," she said, "but you won't frighten me into a stoppage of the heart. I'm not easy to frighten, not as easy as that poor Joss Kift you told about. Don't expect me to be the one who'll have a stoppage of the heart."

Another of her laughs, and I reckon she stepped away from the hole in the door. I didn't look hard to see, I wasn't about to pay her air more mind than I had already. There was a whispery sound of cloth, and I reckoned she'd pulled the wall hanging over the locked door.

I saw that book on the table again. It was big, with thick black covers, like what you might could call a ledger to keep accounts in. What was it a-doing in there with me? I pulled the chair over to the table and hiked up the front cover.

Inside, the pages were good, thick, creamy-colored paper, and on the very front one had been written in dark red ink:

MY BOOK OF THE BLACK ART
by
TIPHAINE

All that in big script letters, but clear and easy to read. Below, in the same writing but smaller:

Read me, if you dare to read, if you dare to know, if you dare to understand. My book is made up of things not dreamed of by ordinary men and women. It is not for cowards but for the brave, not for slaves but for the free; not for fools, but for those who would become wise. *Probatum.*

If she'd left that book on purpose, it must have been for what she reckoned was a good reason. I looked on to what was at the bottom of the page:

But before you read on, make sure to kiss the book

Here

X

Gentlemen, do you all know that for a second I thought I might could do that. But I didn't. I shut the book up again and pushed my chair back and got up. I paced off the room— six paces the long way, four the way across. If my old army stride scale was still right, that made the place fifteen by ten, as I've said. Back I went, and sat down as before.

When I'm alone with naught else to work at, I most always pick guitar. I wished I had mine just then, just to be a-doing. I thought on a whole bunch of songs I liked, and hummed one of them over.

"Maybe I can help you, John."

Sure enough that was Tiphaine again, back outside the door hole.

"Do you miss your guitar?" she inquired me, with the laugh in her voice.

I was up quick and against my side of the door. I must have scowled up my forehead, a-wondering myself how she read my mind.

"I listened to you humming, and sympathized," she said. "Here, this is something that's been on a shelf in this house for years."

"A guitar?" I asked, and I set myself to be ready if she opened the door to put it through. Because then I'd be out.

"It will be a guitar if you're the man I think you are," I heard her say. "If you can put it together. Here, John, pull it through to you."

She had hiked open the slot, and now she shoved through the end of a red velvet bag. "Pull gently," she said. "Gently. Take care that nothing breaks."

It was a right tight fit at that, to drag it through the narrow slot. I heard bits of wood a-rattling inside. It took us better than a minute to work it into my prison, with me to pull and Tiphaine to push and feed. Finally I stood up with the red velvet bag in my hand. It was full of what I reckoned must be kindling wood. I couldn't guess how the whole thing had squeezed through that little small slot, and again Tiphaine seemed like as if she'd read my mind.

"Simply done," said her voice, a-mocking at me. "When the bag was on its way through, I said a word or two to widen the space enough. Don't you wish you knew those words, John? If you did, they might help you out of there. Just as a word or two of your own would do it."

I looked at the slot. If it had been widened for a second, it was narrow now. My arm wouldn't have gone through. I looked at the red velvet sack.

"Go on, untie the string," she bade me. "Open it. Are you afraid? Do you think that perhaps I put a deadly snake in it for you? What are you muttering about in there?"

Half under my breath, I was a-saying a prayer the best I could call it to mind, from the *Long Lost Friend* book; "The blessing from heaven upon all mankind be on me, make my enemies fail before me, that none shall harm me, in the name of the holy power of heaven."

And I hoped that was right enough to the words of the book I wished I had with me, and then I untied the string and opened the bag and shook it out on the floor tiles.

There were thin strips of brown wood, and slices of lighter

wood, and little scraps. There was a bunch of steel strings
sort of looped together into a roll. I picked up some of the
chunks and studied them. I fitted a few of them together,
pegs on one piece into holes on another. They could build
into the neck of a sure-enough guitar. I worked more pieces
into shape.

"Do you still persist in thinking I'm your enemy?" came
Tiphaine's words. "You seem skillful in putting that guitar
together. It will help you pass your time, it may even sweeten
your suspicious nature. Now, I'll leave you for a time, but I'll
return with other things you'll undoubtedly welcome."

Again I heard her feet a-going away.

When all the wood pieces were fitted snug together, I un-
wound the strings and fitted them on, one by one. But before
I went to tune them, I turned the bottom side up to see if it
had air a bad sign on it. There was none such. I got out my
pocket knife and scratched me a cross on the wood. Then, in
case it would help, I cut on each arm of the cross a name of
one of the four rivers that, it says in the book of Genesis,
flowed out of Eden. Pison, Gihon, Hedikiel and Euphrates.
That was something else I'd heard tell can help when you're
a-being conjured, so maybe they might could make the guitar
all right. Finally I did tune the strings up and tried me a
chord or two. It had a pretty good tune, though nowhere near
so good as my own old guitar with the silver strings.

Finally I sat down to pick. A song came into my mind:

> She came down the stair,
> Combing back her yellow hair,
> And her cheeks were as red as the rose . . .

That was the song I always thought for Evadare. How
different from Tiphaine's black wings of hair. But wouldn't I
be better off with a hymn?

There was a good one I knew from a long way back, the

one sung by the Kimber clan up in the Sky Notch country, when they had them a baptizing; a song full of meaning:

> My Lord, what a morning,
> When the stars begin to fall,
> You'll wish you had salvation
> When the stars begin to fall . . .

I sang that one all the way through, verse after verse of it, and wondered myself did Tiphaine hark at me, and what did she think if she did.

CHAPTER 13

"Was that song meant to frighten me?" Tiphaine inquired me from the outside. "Was it to make me wish I had salvation on your terms?"

"It so happens I wasn't much a-studying about you in particular," I said, though that wasn't purely the truth.

"You aren't very flattering to me this evening," she teased at me.

"And I don't much study to flatter folks, either," I replied her, and that time I was a-saying a fact. "Flattery's not a thing I hold is honest."

She looked in through the bars at me, impudent-faced and beautiful. "Mordant, aren't you? And here I've come to see if you weren't getting hungry."

"That's one more thing I haven't studied on."

"Well, but it's on toward sundown." I was surprised to hear her say that, for I hadn't felt the time a-running by, and of course most times I don't carry a watch. "Nevertheless, we've brought you something good for your supper," she said. "It was what was cooked for me, and I do hope you enjoy it."

"I do reckon you give right much time and serious thought to good things in this life," I said, and Tiphaine laughed her laugh, like sweet music.

"Ah, you're doing better now. That time you did flatter me. All right, Quill, slide it through to him."

I heard the slot in the door creak open, and a sort of tray of black-enameled metal came through it. I took hold of it and carried it across to the table, and set it down by the book and the bowl with the pale light. There was a white plate, and on it a roasted bird of some kind, all cut up into joints, with a rosy-brown gravy poured over it. Beside that lay two hot rolls and a square of butter, and a little flat bottle corked up tight and put down on its side. There were a silver knife and fork, and a folded paper napkin.

"That's a salmi of woodcock," came Tiphaine's voice from the door, "with shallots minced up in seasoning and red wine for the sauce. And I included a flask of imported tokay, all the way from Hungary—Count Dracula's home country, you know. Enjoy it, John. I must leave you now, to attend to a few trifling details."

I heard the soft stir of her dress as she moved off away. That supper smelt better all the time. I dragged the chair over.

"Don't, John," came a soft whisper at the outside window. "Is she gone? Whatever you do, don't eat that food she gave you."

Quick, I stepped there. One look showed me that nobody was at the hole in the door. I moved close to the window, and there outside the brass bars was Lute Baynor, a-standing on tiptoe to see in.

"I was at work in Tiphaine's kitchen when supper was a-getting ready," she said to me, so soft a voice I had to strain my ears for it. "Tiphaine set up the tray for you with her own hands, and I saw her speak a spell into it and scatter on a pinch of powder."

"What kind of powder?" I inquired her.

"Who knows that? It might could be a love powder, a death powder—all according to what she may wish for you. Don't eat it, John, eat this."

She was a-shoving something in betwixt the bars, all wrapped up in what looked like a piece of printed paper. "All that's there came from a store in the county seat. It won't hurt you. But now—I'd better run."

And she did run like a scared rabbit, in amongst those hazy

bushes. I turned back from the window, went again to look out at the door just in case somebody was a-using round in the big room outside. Then I sat in the chair and unwrapped what Lute had given me.

It was a big, flattened-out roll of white bread. If it had been much bigger it would have been a loaf. A knife had sliced it open, and I took off the top half. There inside was a slice of ham, on top of a slice of yellow cheese, and both halves of the bread looked buttered. I put the thing back together and studied over it.

Lute had allowed that likely some sort of magic had been put on the rations Tiphaine had fetched me. Could she be a-telling just a big story about that, I wondered myself, could maybe the magic truly be on this sandwich. A-trying to make up my mind betwixt Tiphaine and Lute, I spread out the paper that the sandwich had been wrapped up in. It wasn't printed air such a thing, it was a typewritten page. Since then I've kept it, since then I've read it time and time again, and here's what it said:

FROM THE HEART OF THE TEMPLE
Mystic Month, Wondrous Week, Dire Day
ODI SPAEE I
Wolver

PELEZ COMPRONIS

The Spirits rise around us,
The rattling skeleton of the Crimson Serpent now glides in the light of the moon's rays

TOBI! TOBI!! TOBI!!!

Let the watchword go forth and be heard. Advise the trustworthy and no other. Hear the word, and obey

TOBI! TOBI!! TOBI!!!

To all who serve, to all who are faithful, recognize; graves are unmarked, graves are unnumbered, graves will yawn open.

Again and again, remember your sworn and sacred duty. Do not forget or fail, at your peril.

All praise to our great Master at the lowest, through whom the dead shall live and walk and speak.

TOBI! TOBI!! TOBI!!!

by order of Tiphaine REGINA
QN, Adjutandum

You can bet your lily-white neck I read that thing over and over. Might could it be a spell of some kind, put on the sandwich Lute Baynor had reached in to me? But if she'd wanted to spell me, she'd not have done it thattaway, for me to see. I inquired myself if she just hadn't wrapped up the food in whatair paper might have come to hand. This sheet read more or less like a sort of announcement for something a-coming up with the Wolver crowd—maybe even that Grand Sabbat Tiphaine had named to me. On a lot of the stuff in it I couldn't even make a guess about. The business about Mystic Month, Wondrous Week, Dire Day, and the Tobi-Tobi-Tobi put me in mind of the Ku Klux fellows that bust themselves up a-trying to scare folks out of their pants. And it had come out by Tiphaine's order as Regina—queen, that is—and was signed by QN, which likely had to mean Quill Norbury.

I stuck the sheet away and went back to the table to decide what I'd eat for my supper.

I said it to myself that if I had to choose who'd be the most likely to poison or conjure me, it would purely have to be Tiphaine. She had it up her lovely nose to do something with me. About Lute Baynor, the worst I could be was suspicious. So I carried that good-smelling tray into the bathroom and flushed down all the food and poured out the last drop of the wine. I went back to the door with the tray and plate and slid them out through the slot. They jangled loud on the floor out yonder, but nobody moved in the big room. It must be empty. Back to the table, I out with my old pocket knife and opened it and cut the sandwich in two. As I picked up a big half in my hand, I recollected a blessing of thanks I'd learned when I was a boy, and I said it over inside myself.

That, I figured, might do some good, and I couldn't think of aught else. I was right hungry by then, and bit into the sandwich. The bread and butter and ham and cheese were all good. I finished the one half of it and tucked up the other in the typewritten paper and slid it under the cot bed for when I'd be bound to want something later on. In the bathroom I took a drink of water, with the hope and prayer it wasn't conjured, too. Once more I sat down and waited awhile to see if what I'd eaten would make me feel different air way. It didn't. It must be all right, and Lute Baynor must be all right, too, for what reason I'd yet to find out. But it made me feel a little tad better to think that not all that range of Wolver people wished me bad luck.

A-trying to figure on Lute Baynor, I recollected what the government man had said about her—how smart she'd figured she was to run off from her folks, and so on like that. Now, maybe she'd come to wish she hadn't. I could guess how just a halfway pretty girl might not truly love a beautiful queen of a woman like Tiphaine, at least not all the way. It just might could be I'd found me a friend and well-wisher. Just then, I reckoned I sure enough needed one.

From the door hole across the room, a voice I'd come to know right well: "John?"

"Yes," I said, and nair looked round from where I sat.

"Did you enjoy your supper? I hope so."

"Yessum, I enjoyed it good enough," I decided to say back.

"And how do you feel?"

"Why, as to that, I feel a trifle cramped up in here."

"That's too bad. All you need to get out is to ask. Ask politely. I can even help you by telling you what words to say."

"You mean, beg to you?" I said. "No, ma'am, I thank you. I'll get out of here my own way."

She laughed. "That's what you think, my friend. Keep thinking it, if it gives you comfort. Because that thinking is erroneous. Now I must say good night, and sleep well."

I heard her as she walked away, a-rustling her dress again. I hadn't got out of my chair, hadn't even looked toward the door when she'd made that talk through the barred hole. After while, I picked up that pegged-together guitar and strummed it to sing me a few songs. I recollect that they were "Little Mathy Groves" and "Driver's Boy," amongst others, and those are right scary songs, with bloody last verses to them. I wondered myself who it was had made up such songs, and why folks liked to hear them so much.

Outside, the light of day was a-fading dim. I went over to the window to look. Seemed like to me as if there was something on the move amongst the trees and brush—I didn't know what, only that it didn't much seem like a human being. I came back to the table, where the light from the bowl seemed like to grow strong, and I looked at the big black book there.

I love books all times, and read in them when I can, but Tiphaine would nair have left that with me except for some reason. Was it to scare me, maybe scare me into a-coming over to her side? Was it a dare to me? I'd said that I'd nair taken a dare yet. With that thought, I flung back the cover.

I could see to read the first page again, and I turned that without a-kissing the place marked for me to kiss.

More round, clear writing, in ink so dark red it looked like dried blood:

THE SALUTATION

All praise be unto the One and Veritable Spirit
of our life and joy and service, which is the strength
and soul of man and woman, the essence of every true
god that is or has been on Earth from the beginning:
And afterward:

You who continually bestow knowledge and force
from age unto age, you whom we have worshipped from
the morning of Time in the groves and in the
meadows, upon high places and deep in caves and
caverns, from age to age, through risings and
wanings of earthly peoples and nations;

Whom still we worship in the midst of mankind's
thronged places and secretly in our houses, in our
temples, whom we worship within our hearts and minds
and souls and bowels;

Who is made manifest in the wisdom and worth of
those who have adored you and have shown your glory
unto those made able to see—these your servants:

Imbra and Loki and Pan and Kalu, and Tetragrammaton
of old; Huitzilopochtli, worshipped in the flowing blood
of thousands; Yama, Dis, Pluto with Persephone his queen,
Set, Surtur and Agni, who by your will and decree rule
the deep-kindled abysses of fire; those great
enchantresses, Medea and Daya and Thaukt and Scylla
and Circe; those dreadful wonders, Chimera and Basilisk
and Medusa and Apis and Geryon and Yeti and
Gogmagog and Mimir.

And also these, in human guise:

Krishna, Alwax, Kali, Priapus, Khem and Amoun and
Mentu; Simon Magus, Abramelin, Merlin, Nostradamus,
Jacob Boehme, Eliphas Lévi, Albertus Magnus,
John Dee, Edward Kelly, Simon Forman, Miles Robeck,
Daniel Dunglas Home; Grigori Efimovich called Rasputin,
and Aleister Crowley. All these famed and flaming
children of the Lion and the Bat and the Serpent, and
how many great others, how many!

Yet this much is but an invocation and a preface to
the wonders you may come to perform as you read onward
in this book.

There, that was the bottom of the writing on the second page. I thought it over. If the book had been put there to make me scared, it hadn't yet done that, it only made me curious. The pale light from the bowl flashed and sent up a couple of white sparks. I felt the darkness in round me, like as if there was something or other sneaked into the room with me. I near about heard a breathing, but maybe that was the blood a-beating in my ears. I wondered all over that list of names. I'd heard only a few of them. After a second or so more, I turned to the next page of red ink writing:

THE FIRST INSTRUCTION

As the Master Therion, the Beast 666, Aleister
Crowley, has fearlessly proclaimed, Magic is the most
sublime, and at the same time the most discredited, of
all studies. It is derided and persecuted, but it
prevails. Let the scoffer depart, let the true
believer continue.

Magic is the science and practice of causing
Nature to move and perform and obey and serve
as your Will commands.

All acts of the Will, understandingly performed,
are Magical acts.

One who properly seeks to do what he Wills has the
whole force of the Universe to guide, uphold and serve
him.

Those who decry Magic are fatuous and limited in
understanding. They themselves know nothing of the
nature of the Universe.

But he who knows Magic as hereinafter interpreted
and exampled may command and move the Universe to do
his will. But first he must fit himself for this
triumphant task. He must be wholly sufficient unto
himself and must establish himself in the proper relation
between himself and the Universe.

Others have successfully accomplished these things;
and what man or woman has done, man or woman can do.
Then proceed with prayerful care. You must call for
help, in the wonderful names heretofore provided to you.
But call on no name without cause or consideration.
For those who are summoned to you must know for what
purpose they are summoned, or they will punish you with
suffering. You will feel their claws, their fangs, if
you have been so fatally foolish as to appeal to them.

Thus you begin

THE SECOND INSTRUCTION

Look on the page before this and speak aloud the
names of wonder catalogued there.

I slammed the book shut, slammed it hard.

For the air of the room made a whispery sound like as if
there was talk about me in it, almost like as if my name was
spoken. Right then and there it seemed to me that, if I
turned round where I sat, I'd see things there, in the dark
behind me and next to me. See what?

I wondered myself what must I do. The only thing I could
bring to mind was a spell I'd heard once, and I said it the
best I could recollect in my mind, not a-speaking air word out
loud:

*Three false tongues have bound me, but three holy
tongues have spoken for me. Heaven is above me, Earth
is beneath me, and I am between. Heaven's blessing be
here and all here and all round about me, amen.*

All at once quick then, the air didn't feel so tight, so heavy.
It was just a tad brighter in the room. Now I made myself to
look round and behind. Naught was there, only those
smooth, blue walls. Though I thought I heard a little sort of
racket in the leaves outside. Maybe it wasn't aught more than
a breath of wind.

Voices again, but from outside the door this time, from something in the big room there. I went to see if I could hark at them. I figured that Tiphaine and some others were at the big table, with business to talk over, but I couldn't make out air word they said.

After while, I tramped back across the tiled floor and to the bathroom. Enough light reached in there for me to wash my face and neck and hands good. Then I went to the bed and laid myself down on top of the blankets without even a-bothering to pull off my boots.

It had been quite a day I'd had for myself. I tried to guess what Simon would think when I hadn't come back to the cabin. I hoped to high heaven he wouldn't try to come a-searching for me into Wolver and likely get caught his own self. And I tried to figure on the government man in the auto court in the county seat, if he had air notion in the world what to do.

Thoughts like that, I reckoned, would keep me awake for hours. But they did no such thing. Enough had happened to tire me out, and I slid off into sleep.

CHAPTER 14

I say that I went to sleep, but I sure enough didn't sleep well.

Times are when I reckon I've mostly slept my best when I was camped somewhere outside, like when I was there amongst the yews and laurels by the stream outside Wolver. I'd rested all right in Simon's cabin, too, but likely that came because I was purely tired out then, had been in a bad fight and got myself punched and kicked and all like that. And of course Simon's friendship and his good talk had been mightily helpful. But here I was all alone, in a little prison room of a place with a bare dark floor and bare pale walls, shut in from the sky and the outside air. The light from the bowl made dancy shadows on the ceiling. And so, well, I nair did rest easy. To this day I wonder myself if the dreams I had were sure enough dreams, or something real, at least something wakeful.

It started out thissaway. I dropped off, but I tossed and tumbled, and then I started and sat up. Something was in the room with me, a great big something that sort of hung up above my bed. I thought it was like a black bull, or at least something like a bull, but yet in some ways like a bear. Maybe its feet were like a bear's feet, if I truly saw them. I thought it glittered its eyes at me and they were someway white eyes, and it sort of grumbled at me in its throat. Horns and long ears were to its head, seemed like to me. I tried to say something or other, and then I was broad waked up and whatair the thing might could have been was gone.

Only, it wasn't quite gone. Something like it still hung and

faced there, maybe like a ghost of the big dark shape of it.
And I dug my hand across my eyes and sat up straighter, and
there was naught there now, naught but the cold, creepy
remembry of it.

And meanwhile that pale light from the silver bowl shone
itself and made its dance and flicker. It was no easy trick to
go back to sleep, but I stretched out my legs and slacked my
muscles and some way I managed to do it.

Then, I was wide awake and a-tingling again. I wondered
what was in the room with me, and I looked and I saw.

Or maybe I didn't rightly see it, just felt it. Felt like as if a
big snake, bigger than air snake in this world had air been,
was in the room with me.

I lay there like a man paralyzed. My notion of the thing
was that it was red-colored—hadn't that paper with the sandwich spoken something about a Crimson Serpent? And it
seemed to move and sway, lift its head, and there was a
sound in the air of a heavy chain that somebody was maybe
a-dragging on the tiled floor.

If it bothers you all to hear me name that thing, you all
can guess how it fixed me. I lay and goggled. If I'd told
Tiphaine I couldn't be scared, that was a lie right then. The
big coils seemed like to fill up the room, and clear and plain I
saw the flat head come up above them. A shallow, jowly
head, trowel-shaped like the head of a snake chuck full of
poison, with watching eyes, bright and black and nasty.

Then I sat up straight. "Mercy of God!" I hollered at it.

It faded out, like the bull-thing I'd seen, and I was too glad
to be surprised. It went off away from there, though I halfway reckoned I smelled a snaky odor on the air round me. I
got up out of the bed, glad, glad to be alone in my prison
room.

I looked at the light on the table and the book beside it.
There, I told myself, that was what had done those things,
had almost done them to me. I'd been gone gump enough to

look into that book, just the way Tiphaine had counted on me to look. If I'd kept on a-reading into it, what for hell's sake, what would have happened then?

All right, the thing had been my stupid doing, even if I hadn't gone to do it. So I'd better undo it some way. If I'd read in the book, I must unread it if so be there was such a thing to do.

Unread it . . . there, that was the answer. Once a fellow named Embro Hallcott had told me about how somebody took off a spell of magic by a-reading it backward. And weren't witches supposed to do their conjures by a-saying the Lord's Prayer backward? Would it work?

Only one way to find out.

I sat down and opened the book, as careful as though I expected to burn my fingers on it. I turned that first page and the second. The third had been the last I'd looked at. I went to the bottom writing, and started with the lowest line of it, and I read it upward, line by line, like this:

names of wonder catalogued there.
Look on the page before this and speak aloud the
THE SECOND INSTRUCTION
Thus you begin

I'll be dogged if upside down it didn't make some crazy sense that wasn't the whole way crazy. Up and up and up, a line at the time, with the sweat a-running down my face, I read the thing:

you have been so fatally foolish as to appeal to them.
suffering. You will feel their claws, their fangs, if
purpose they are summoned, or they will punish you with
For those who are summoned to you must know for what
But call on no name without due cause or consideration.
help, in the wonderful names heretofore provided to you.
Then proceed with prayerful care. You must call for

Strange as all that sounds, it someway added up to a promise of help. Help was what it kept a-saying. I kept on with the rest of the page up to the top, and closed the book again.

I felt relaxed. Tired out, the way you'd have thought I'd been a-grubbing up stumps in a field. I got up, and my legs kind of bobbled as I headed back to the bed and lay down. When I breathed, I didn't any more get the snaky smell in the air. Under my breath I said a whole bunch of holy names that I figured had maybe helped me, and after while I did sleep, though it wasn't a sound sleep, not a restful one. But I was purely grateful for what sleep it was.

For hours I dozed and tossed and came up from it, and it wasn't yet sunrise when I got up and washed myself good and reached under the bed for what was left of Lute Baynor's big sandwich. The paper it was wrapped in, with that word about the Crimson Serpent on the move, I folded up and stuck in my pocket to keep, and I found myself right ready to eat the bread and cheese and meat. Afterward, I took a chance and drank water in the bathroom. It didn't seem to do aught to me. Then, back to the chair and I picked up the guitar and tried to make me up a song:

> Nobody here in this little room,
> Nobody here but me,
> I'm by myself but I'm with myself
> And that's how I'm apt to be;
> Out yonder the sun's a-rising up,
> A-shedding its foggy light,
> And on time goes, and nobody knows
> Where I'm likely to be tonight.

"Very tuneful," said Tiphaine's voice at the door, "but you're most likely to be right where you are now, John. And how did you sleep? Did you have dreams, perhaps?"

"A couple–three of those," I replied her. "None of them about you."

"I could wish you had dreamed of me. Sweetly. How do you feel this fine morning?"

"Why," I said, "all right."

"Good," she said, like as if she truly cared. "Since you're awake, breakfast will be along soon. How would you like a cheese omelet and hot toast and coffee?"

"No, I thank you, ma'am," I said. "I don't rightly think I care aught for breakfast today."

"That's too bad." I reckoned her red lips rounded themselves to say that. "I hope that last night's supper didn't disagree with you."

"Likely you took you some trouble a-fixing that supper for me," I said, "but no, what I ate didn't pester me at all."

"No? And you feel contented by yourself, with yourself?"

"Stone walls do not a prison make," I quoted, "nor iron bars a cage."

She laughed about that. "You know the Cavalier poets, at least you know Richard Lovelace. Education, even sophistication—I promise myself some rewarding talks with you. Perhaps you'll educate yourself even more, with the book I left for you. All right, just as you say about breakfast, but I think you'd have enjoyed the omelet."

She went a-rustling away. I walked over and looked out through the barred window.

"John," whispered Lute Baynor from under the sill. "Here, quick, I fetched you something."

In through the bars she reached it to me, and scurried out of sight in the brush. I unwrapped the paper, just brown store paper this time. It was another great big sandwich, made of a piece of corn pone split through and filled in with thick slices of fried bacon and a leaf of lettuce. I slid it under the bed, as I'd done with the food the day before, to save for later in the evening.

Then what would I do to kill time. There wasn't air luck if I read in that book Tiphaine had mentioned, I'd had my possible full of that kind of reading. For a second I thought I might could call out at the door and inquire Tiphaine if she had a newspaper for me to read. Even what they'd print at the county seat would be all right; there would be lots of interesting items about who had some nice veal calves or a nice short-corn crop a-coming along, or just a bad head cold. But I wasn't about to ask Tiphaine even such a small favor as that, didn't want to owe her aught. So I dug out the typewritten sheet and looked at it one more time.

Big doings were a-going to come, and quick. Tiphaine had named it about three days, and a day and a night were gone, which left only two. Call it some forty-odd hours left for me to figure myself out of there and off somewhere yonder in the open. All it would take was the right figuring. A simple matter of rationalization, as once I'd heard Preacher Frank Ricks put it. If I'd said that thing to Tiphaine, she'd have laughed and called me educated again. She seemed like as if she relished that joke about my education, if it was a joke.

I sort of reviewed over all I'd heard tell, all I'd guessed. I wanted to do some more thinking about it. Now and then, I've found I thought best when I was a-walking. So I walked.

It was six paces the long way of the room, four paces across the short way. From one corner to the far one, it was seven paces and a tad more. I stepped it off again and again and yet again, and all the while I thought.

I decided the best I could about this Wolver settlement, that one time it had been just a little small mill village, like lots of others here and there in these lands. And it had come to be a nest of creepy folks, all caught up in their old worship of devils, and a-raising their poor sorry little baby children to believe in the same thing. Tiphaine was the life and heart of the thing, that was plain to see. On her own word, seemed like as if she'd had another name once and likely chances to do something with it, but she'd come and holed up here for what she sure enough felt were good reasons enough. And by now I had proof, plenty of proof, that she could do a big sight of things with charms and spells and so on.

But the main point was those foreign fellows that were due to come to the big Sabbat business. My friend from the government bureau had told me that, and Tiphaine herself had talked about them. Up and down I walked, six steps, four across, four back, six again and seven slantways. What foreign parts would they be from? I could make up my mind what countries hated this one the most. It seemed like to me as if most countries do hate one another, and keep out of wars because both sides, or all sides, are purely bound to lose the next war.

But what was a right peculiar thing was, though I was bound to be in a bad fix there, I didn't feel like a man in a bad fix. It was cramped in that room, it was lonesome, and I felt I had big things to do outside, important things. But I wasn't outright scared, the way I'd been when the bull-animal and the red snake had showed themselves the night before.

Who were the foreign fellows who were due to come, I inquired myself again, and what would they have to do with Tiphaine, and how could I get away and tell the tale? I walked and I walked, a good hour maybe. I must have done miles in that room, six paces and four paces and seven paces at a time. Yet I hadn't an answer to my problem of how to get out and talk where it would do the world some good.

At last I sat myself down and looked at the table, with its bowl of light and the book. Again I made myself the promise I wouldn't dip into Tiphaine's book of black magic. And I recollected how she'd said for me not to fool round with the light. And that one time, at least, I felt I could take her at her word.

"John?" somebody hailed me from the door. It wasn't Tiphaine this time, it was a man's voice, sort of respectful-sounding. I got up and went there and looked through the bars. It was Quill Norbury, dressed up in his good-looking blue suit.

"What you want of me?" I inquired him. "Did you come here to let me out?"

"I can't do that, John, though I wonder if it wouldn't be best for us all if I did. If I let you out and told you good-bye and saw no more of you."

"What you want of me?" I said again.

"Tiphaine's disappointed in you," said Quill Norbury. "She says that you refuse to listen to what she tries to tell you for your own good."

"That's because I don't reckon it's for my own good."

"She's asked me to come and reason with you. Here, she sends you this."

What he poked in at me betwixt the bars was yellow and had a glow to it. I figured it was about the size of a pack of cigarettes.

"No, I thank you," I told him. "Take it back to her."

"But it's gold, John." He sounded like as if he begged to me. "It's pure gold. It's yours."

"Tell her I won't take it. Won't touch it."

"It's yours," he said again. "Tiphaine gives it to you. At the price of gold today, it's worth a small fortune. And we could show you where there's more, lots more."

He shoved it on through and it fell and clanked on the tiles. I knelt down and looked at the little chunk. Then I fished out a handkerchief and put it over the thing and picked it up without a touch of my fingers. It felt as heavy as lead, must have weighed at a couple of pounds. I jumped up and walked over to the window and flung it out there. Something went a-scuttling away, like a dog when you heave a rock at it.

"I didn't take it," I said over my shoulder. "Didn't put my hand to it. Tell Tiphaine I got rid of it out the window. Why for hell's sake do I mean so much to you that you want to buy me at a price like that?"

"It was only a present to you," he said. "I'd estimate that much gold to be worth thousands of dollars. Many times that amount can be yours for the asking."

"That's not what I ask," I said back to him.

"Quill," came the voice of Tiphaine, "you don't seem to be handling this business at all well. Once or twice lately, in this way or that, you've been a disappointment to me. Let me talk to John."

"Aw," he sort of whined, and went out of sight away from the bars. Tiphaine's face came there instead of his. She shook her head at me, slow and, in a way, sad. Her black hair rippled.

"I'm beginning to wonder what I'm to do with you," she halfway mourned.

"Try a-turning me loose from here," I said.

"You know I don't dare do that, at this stage."

"No," I agreed her, "I reckon you don't dare do that."

"When you go free, you go as a high and honored figure among us."

"That wouldn't be a-going free," I said.

"John," she said, and her voice went sharper, "I've done my best to show patience about your case. I told you when first you went in there that I gave you three days. The second of those three is coming to its close, and that will leave you only one more day. Hasn't the light on the table there shone a little into your darkness, pointed you to wisdom and clarity?"

"You told me not to fool with that light," I reminded her, "and I haven't."

"Then you believe me, for once. That's an encouraging sign. To believe is to trust, and to trust is to love, isn't that so?"

"How am I a-going to love somebody who keeps me locked up?" I asked. "Whatever trust is, you don't trust me."

"Trust will come, John. You have perhaps twenty-four hours to learn to trust in me, to let me have trust in you. But it's getting near suppertime."

"Nothing for me," I said, right quick. "If it's just the same."

"You're still observing your fast, then. I'll leave you to it."

She went, and Quill Norbury went with her, and I watched them go. Then I got out my sandwich and ate the top half of the pone and a couple of bacon chunks, cold but crisp, and a part of the lettuce. I put the rest back for my breakfast. A rustle at the window, and I went and looked out.

"John?" said Lute Baynor. "I fetched you these."

It was a little china cup with strawberries in it. "I grew them my own self," she said. "Now, I'd better go."

I had those strawberries, and they were as sweet as sugar candy. I put the empty cup under the bed. I walked a little while more, up and down and across the room. Then I washed up all over and put my clothes on again and lay on the bed. I crossed my ankles one over the other and put my hands together behind my head and looked up at the pale ceiling. I gave the whole business a good think one more time, then I did what I could to get to sleep. I counted, counted, counted, must have got up into the four or five hundreds and then at last I dropped off.

Naught to wake me up then, though I did have dreams. I thought I saw a wagon a-driving past, all closed in so you couldn't see who it was held the reins, but instead of horses to draw it there were wolves. They were big as horses, with red eyes and tongues. Then things changed, and I thought I was in an almighty big city somewhere. Seemed like to me I stood on the sidewalk by a big wide street, farther across than a football field. It was full of traffic a-going both ways, little bitty cars, I couldn't tell what make they were. In the middle of the street, where you'd expect some sort of parkway, it was wide and had houses in it, with trees a-growing up by their doors. Over that you could see big high buildings on the far side, and past them, long past them, higher ones. I thought I looked at big tall towers miles away, but clear in the air, clear as a-looking at far-off mountains.

A dream like that, I sometimes figure, is a look at some city the way it will be maybe lifetimes from now. It might could be, in our sleep we see into what's to come. But that night I didn't see aught of the future to tell me how to get out of that prison where I'd been flung.

Yet all the time that night I did sleep, or if I woke up it was only a little small part of the way, to sink back again. Somehow the coming of morning outside got my eyes open at last.

Out of the bed I got up and drank water and washed up in the bathroom and came back. As it had been before, Tiphaine spoke through the bars.

"After a hungry day and night, what do you think of breakfast this morning? I can promise you fresh-caught trout and fruit bread toasted and buttered, and some coffee you'll say is the best you ever drank."

"I won't be a-drinking it," I said, "so I won't be able to say air such thing."

"Just how long do you intend to carry out this holy fast?" she asked. "This starving of yourself?"

"Why," I made answer, "I've heard tell that the doctors have it that a man can go ten days without food and won't perish to death, won't even feel a bad harm."

"Ten days," she repeated me. "I've already said, John, that there won't be ten days to spend in this business. Midnight tonight is zero hour. Now excuse me, and try to see the sense in what I've told you."

She went away. I hadn't looked at her the one time, but I went now to be dead sure that she was out of sight. Then I got what was left of the food Lute Baynor had fetched, and ate it. It went down all right. Bacon and corn bread always suit me.

Afterward, I toured the room and the bathroom all over, tested the walls and found they were so solid they didn't even echo. I looked at the brass bars at the window and in the door hole and figured they couldn't be howked out of there without some kind of acetylene torch. I studied the end of the key that stuck through the lock on my side, and wondered myself if I had some sort of wrench or vise, could I maybe turn it. Again I wound up with the thought that I couldn't get out by myself. And Tiphaine had given me just the rest of the day and up to the midnight that was a-coming. Then, the way she'd half said it, would be my finish. That, or holler out to her that I quit, that I'd do whatair it was she wanted me to do, without even a good guess as to what it might could be.

All right, and did that scare me? I'd been scared night before last, by those shadowy things, the bull and the snake, but it's the unknown that purely scares you. About death, I'd been so close to death time after time that I could count the teeth in the skull face. I didn't feel it was a specially unusual thing, death. I hoped, though, that if it came this time it would be quick and fairly easy. I'd come along to where I hoped just that one thing.

Right then, weakness came over me, and I sort of stumbled to the chair and sat down. My head swam a little bit, and my ears sort of popped. A moment of that, and the feeling went away and I got up again.

"How did that feel, John?" Tiphaine inquired me from the big room. "I was experimenting. I touched my wand to your image, and you felt it all the way in there. Which proves I've succeeded in connecting your life to the image. That makes it convenient for tonight's activity."

"Why don't you just finish me off?" I dared her.

"That would be a trifle premature. Midnight of the Sabbat is the proper moment, with all signs right. I'm reconciled to that. I'm disappointed in you, but I've learned to bear disappointments."

"You'll be stuck with my dead body," I said. "It's a pretty big body to be a-lying round dead. Damaging evidence, don't you reckon?"

"Not if we burn it up, and use the ashes in charms."

She went away, and I heard a sort of hiss at the window, and went there. Lute Baynor was outside. She shoved me in two eggs and a cold biscuit and ran off again, the way she always did. When I cracked the eggs, they came out hard-boiled. I ate them and the biscuit and drank some water.

More noise in the big room beyond the door. I went to look, but the curtain was drawn. There was talk out there, likely round the table. I heard a man say something in what sounded like French, though not like a Frenchman a-saying it. Tiphaine talked back to him in the same language. Then what I figured was Quill Norbury asked, "What was that?" and Tiphaine said, "He prepares to honor his government's promise if we honor ours." Another man's voice, and Tiphaine translated, "He was only paying me a rather graceful compliment, Quill." And more talk, and more. I sat and guessed about it, since I couldn't much understand it.

Finally, and the sun was on the way down outside, Tiphaine came and pulled back the curtain outside the door hole. I looked out at her. Behind her stood Quill Norbury and two other men, a chunky one and a wispy one, both dressed right up to the nines beyond the nines in costly-looking summer suits. Tiphaine held that wax dummy of me in her arms, held it like a girl with a toy doll baby.

"Good-bye, John," she said. "My guests and I will go out to dine *alfresco,* and I want to take a last leave of you, because when I get back you'll be gone."

"I do hope I will," I said, a-wondering myself how to work it.

"I'm taking this image as a souvenir of you," she said. "You may sit here and watch the light in the bowl. Whatever happens to the image will happen to the light—and to you."

"I see," I said.

"You don't really see, but you will. Good-bye, John," she said again.

Away she rustled, out of sight. The big room was still.

Whatever lights had shone in that room had been doused out, and I could see naught there. I heard the door to the hall close. She'd left me alone, all right, all of them had left me alone. I went back to the window. It was sundown. Maybe the last sundown I'd air see.

"John?" came my whispered name, a deep man's voice from under the sill.

"Who the hell are you?" I asked.

"Not so loud. This is Simon Latchney. Here, take this paper of dust. When you put it on the lock in there, the lock will open."

CHAPTER 15

"What's this stuff you've fetched me?" I inquired him.

"Dust to put on the lock, I told you. Don't stop to talk, put it on and it will open up the door and you can get out. Nobody's in the house just now—we watched all of them leave and walk on up the street out there."

"We?" I said after him. "Who's we?"

"I'll tell you everything when you're out of there. Hurry up, now."

He bobbed back out of sight in the deepening dusk.

In the light from the bowl I studied the twist of paper he had given me, and carefully I prized it open. Inside were a few pinches, not so much as a handful, of grainy stuff like brown meal. As Simon had bade me do, I walked across the tiles and dabbed the stuff into the lock, just below where the end of the key stuck out on my side.

A second, and then the lock gave out a sort of rattly groan. I heard tumblers go click-click inside it. When I pushed, the door swung open before me.

One last look I shot all round the room where I'd been a prisoner. I wasn't leaving aught behind me, except that cup. On the table flickered the light in the bowl, and there was that book of Tiphaine's. I didn't reckon on a-taking them with me—I believed Tiphaine about the light, and I'd had all the study of the book I felt I wanted forever. Glad as glad, I stepped through the open door and pushed the hanging aside. There I was, out in Tiphaine's big sitting room.

Gentlemen, it was right dim in there and nair movement

in it, but I could make out the big table. The little wax dummy made to look like me, it was gone. I'd seen it in Tiphaine's arms. I crossed the floor to the door beyond, and it stood open. Out I went, into the front hall. The Earth Mother statue wasn't where it had been, likely they'd taken it to their Sabbat business. I opened the big front door. It skreeked when I pulled. As I stepped out, I felt freedom set in on me. Just beside the steps waited Simon. He had on his old army shirt with camouflage leaves, good for moonlight in the woods.

"Here," he said quickly. "Come through these bushes at the side. We mustn't go out at the front gate, all the people in Wolver are walking along the street."

He led me round the corner of the house into a thickety mess of leaves. Too dark to see plain there, but I reckoned it was a hell of laurel. He made a *psst* sound through his teeth, and it was answered from up ahead. We struggled through to a more open place amongst bushes and trees, with the house a-looming up in the light of the big cloudy moon. There stood somebody.

"You made it away, John," murmured Lute Baynor's voice.

As we came close, I saw that her face was all drawn and wide-eyed, like as if she was far gone in a scare. She wore a long, dark dress or gown, and her hair was blown round to the sides of her face. "Thank God, you're safe so far," she said. "There, I said the name of God and it was no pain to me to say it."

I wondered twenty things about her, but Simon was a-pushing through what looked to be a stand of hemlock. Beyond, the three of us knelt under some low branches, and from there we could see into the street.

Simon was right. The whole Wolver crowd seemed to be afoot out yonder. They sort of marched along by twos and threes, closed up into a column, and they all looked to have blackish robes. I could pretty much make out which were men and which were women, and little children were along there, too, and nair one of them a-making a sound. That is, they didn't talk. But you could hear their feet, scrape-scrape, on the gravel. I wanted to ask some questions, but I sure enough didn't want to be heard if I asked one of them.

They must be headed for the tumbledown church. If Tiphaine and her guests had left before I got out, likely they were at the church already. And something was due to happen to me there that night. I looked up at the blurry moon and figured that I had hours to keep it from a-happening.

But Lute spoke, though it was so soft I had to strain my ears to hear. "I'm supposed to be there with them," she whispered. "A-going with them."

"Why aren't you?" I asked, close to her so she could hear.

"I had to do something first—something to help you. What they expect of me tonight—"

Simon waved his dark hand at us to make us keep quiet.

Gentlemen, I reckoned that while I might could be out of my prison, I wasn't yet out of the woods; and just then, with that procession a-using along out in the street, I'd do well to stay in the woods a spell.

"Look, yonder at the end," Lute was a-whispering in my ear.

The whole parade had sort of petered out. Behind the last two–three of the folks came what first I figured was a bunch of dogs. But it wasn't a bunch of dogs.

I'd seen such things round Wolver. One had horns like a goat, ears like a jackass. Another might could have been a black bear, a-trying to decide whether to walk on two feet or four. Another stirred as it crept along, and I made out that it had leathery wings of some sort, though it didn't fly just then, just looked like as if it was a-getting ready to. I sort of scrunched down lower under the branches and felt glad that the breeze was a-blowing our way so that nothing with a good sense of smell would know we were there.

"Those are familiars," breathed Lute to me.

Familiars, I knew that word. You get you one when you join a witch cult, and they run your errands and help in your conjure work. Long years back, you could get yourself hung to the nearest tree for owning one. I watched them move along after the people. Simon spoke:

"We can follow along too now," he said. "Head for your old camp place, John. We've got to do some talking."

Talking would be bound to help, I reckoned, though I wasn't right sure how. We moved along in the brush beside the road, a-taking care not to rustle a leaf. Lute, I noticed, was good at the making of no noise about that. Out in the road ahead, that column of conjure folks kept on the move until we got near the church grounds. I could see red glow up yonder—a fire would be a-going, and now and then a voice cried out in the night. The crowd we'd followed headed in there, amongst the scrubby bushes and tumbled-over gravestones.

"Let's see if we can get across the road," said Simon.

"One at a time," I said. "First me, then when I'm over yonder and nobody else is in the road, Lute comes and you last, Simon."

"I mustn't go with youins," said Lute, in a voice about to cry. "If I stay away, they'll come to look for me—maybe they'll find youins. I'd better go in there with them."

"Will you be all right there?" I asked her.

"I—oh, I don't know."

She moved off toward the churchyard.

"That poor child's in a bad fix, I sort of guess," said Simon, a-watching her go. "All right, John, you said you'd slip across first."

I looked up and down the road in the red moonlight. Naught moved there. I headed across at a run, stopped on the far side to hark at things. Then I waved my arm, and Simon came quick after me. We slid into the woods and I knew them, even with only a spatter of light. We pulled it all the way to the yews where I'd made my camp. It seemed years since I'd been there. I sat on a rock, and Simon on a half-rotten log.

"However did you know where I was shut up?" I inquired him.

"That Lute Baynor girl came and told me."

I shook my head, a-trying to understand. "Why did she do that? Why would she turn against her own crowd?"

"She wants out of that crowd, John. She can't take any more of what they're telling her she's got to do."

We sat, and he filled me in. Lute had got herself a right much scared by the things that went on in Wolver. Now, with those two foreign agents there, Tiphaine had told her to go off to bed with them. Tiphaine had talked like as if that was an honor to Lute, but Lute had turned sick against it. She'd run all the way to Simon's cabin, just on a wild guess that he and I were friends, and told him about me shut up in the prison room.

"So I asked her, try to get food to you so you wouldn't eat any conjures," he said, "and I went right to work on something to open a lock. It was in a book of spells I remember, and it takes a while, or I'd have come sooner."

"It worked master," I said. "What was it?"

"You kill a green frog, and I hated to do that, but I did. Then you dry it out three days next to a fire, and grind it up into a powder to put in the lock."

"It worked master," I said again. "That charm you recollected is in the old *Grand Albert* book."

"Some such matter." He nodded me. "Now, John, I'd say our best move would be to get you out of here. All the way out of this part of the world."

"No, sir," I said back, and shook my head. "First off, there's Lute Baynor to help out whatair way we can, because she helped me. As you said, she's in a right bad fix, and I owe it to her to stand by her. If she hadn't come and sought you out, I wouldn't be here right now."

"That's a true word," he agreed me. "You say, first off we try to help her. What's to be done second off?"

"Something for my sake, you'd better believe. Because I might could run now, but likely I'd nair be able to run past where that Tiphaine lady could put a hurt on me."

Now it was my time to do some filling in. I named it to Simon about my time in Tiphaine's lockup room; about the book which it wasn't good if you read in it; the light that was supposed to mean my life some way or other; and then all about the little wax figure of me that I'd seen Tiphaine go a-toting away with her to where she meant to do things to it. When I narrated my dreams—or were they sure-enough dreams?—about the bull-thing and the big snake-thing, he crinkled his wise, dark face over it. He looked sad, like as if he'd lost a kinfolk.

"I judge you're smart enough to realize that you're lucky to be alive this minute," he said. "Things like that, coming to visit—they put me in mind of how witch doctors make things happen in Africa, where my folks came from."

"You've studied African things?" I asked.

"I've made it a point to study them. And to believe that they can work, over there and likewise here. Especially something in this country we're in."

"What?"

"Another old Indian tale they tell," said Simon. "About a big red snake in the waters of the Hiwassee River."

"I've heard the same thing," I told him. "It's at a place they used to call Tianusiy, where the Valley River flows down into the Hiwassee. A point of land reaches out there, and that's where the red thing is. Only, the Cherokee men say it's a leech, not a snake. But it can eat people up if they go in."

Simon studied me. "You've been there? You've seen it?"

"I walked out on the point and looked into the water. I saw something that stirred there, but I don't rightly know what. I wasn't air raised to be such a fool as to go in and find out."

It wasn't the comfortablest thing to recollect, so I changed the subject.

"All right," I finished up, "whatair I've been able to do so far to stave off Tiphaine's black magic, that wax image ties in with me, strong and all wrong. She touched her wand to it, and that made me as weak as they say a cat's supposed to be. And she tried twenty different whichaways to make me join up with her, offered me all sorts of things and climbed up on top of them things herself for a bonus. But I'd told her no, and I kept a-telling her no. And sometime tonight, I reckon she'll go about things to wipe me clear off the face of this earth."

"I see," said Simon. "I see. That's right bad, John, but we ought to have a few hours yet. We can go back to the cabin and figure out something to do. You ought to have something hot to eat, first time in three days when you've just had sandwiches, and I'll pour you some wine. I could even say a communion service for it. While you eat, we can decide something, and then head back and see about it."

He was right serious, but right confident. It made me feel better to hear him talk thattaway. We got up and headed along the road. Over yonder at the church, fires danced up high and we heard voices, and the sound of some music. I made out the beat of drums, more drums than one, and the wailing call of some sort of pipe or horn. I wondered just what.

It was good when we got to Simon's cabin, with those shrubs and the horseshoe that should ought to be some protection. He lighted the lamp and the little stove, and fried us salt pork and potatoes, and made coffee. Those things went right well with me, I'm honest to tell you, and likewise I relished my glass of the red wine, though Simon didn't say aught of the communion service, after all. What he did say made good common sense.

This special big-time Sabbat of theirs must be like something he'd studied about, maybe in Jules Michelet, maybe somewhere else. The scholars felt it went back to the beginning of human beliefs, but it was full of throw-offs on all the present religions. Simon had it in mind that when they held one, it sometimes wound up with the death by sacrifice of the principal devil-worshipper. But I couldn't figure that Tiphaine had any notion of a-dying herself.

"No," I said, "she's a-fixing for me to die. She reckons that will be good enough of a finish for their worship business. I'm a-starting to think that she meant that all along, even if I joined them—that I was to die, I mean."

"You're likely in the right about that," Simon agreed me. "So we've got to handle it so that it doesn't happen to you."

I mentioned the flint arrowheads Tiphaine had shown me and how she'd allowed they were elf arrows from the other side of the ocean. "I reckon she means to use them on my wax image," I said. "Use them and kill me in that room in her house where she must think I'm still locked up. And the light in the bowl there will go out then, and I'll be their sacrifice."

"It gives one furiously to think," said Simon.

"What's that you said?" I asked, and he repeated it. He'd heard it, he said, back when he was at the school to learn to be a preacher, and he'd nair forgotten it. "Furiously is the best way to think, sometimes," he said.

"What I can't tell is why they want just my image at the Sabbat," I offered him. "That doesn't strike me as much of a show to put on for visiting folks. You'd figure they'd want to bring me there in person, let them see me die and get sacrificed."

"My notion about that is, they're scared of you," said Simon. "If they took you out of that prison, you'd be just as apt to get away."

"But if they've got the image, wouldn't they use it to kill me no matter where I am?" I argued him. "In the prison place, or right here in your cabin? If I'm free, maybe I have a chance."

"The point is," said Simon, "we won't stay here in my cabin. We'll get out there where they are, put a stop to what they'll do to you before it's done."

"How you figure we're a-going to do that?"

"How?" he repeated me.

But he'd spoken the true word when he said we'd better be there. I tried in my heart to answer that how thing. Finally I looked through my gear and got out the ragged little paperback book I always carried, *The Long Lost Friend*. I turned to page 38, and looked at a diagram of letters printed there, supposed to be copied out on white paper and carried with you, to keep off bad spells. But then I looked at what was on the front page:

Whoever carries this book with him, is safe from all his enemies, visible and invisible. . . .

And well I knew that I had visible and invisible enemies, in carload lots:

And whoever has this book with him cannot die without the holy corpse of Jesus Christ . . .

Which I took to mean, couldn't die without taking communion. It was just as good that Simon hadn't said a service with our wine:

. . . nor drowned in any water, nor burn up in any fire, nor can any unjust sentence be passed upon him. So help me.

And three crosses at the bottom: + + +

Unjust sentence, that was what Tiphaine was a-passing on me, and figured to carry it out. I didn't write on a paper, I just pushed the book down the front of my shirt, down to where it rode against my belt.

"When do we start for there, John?" Simon inquired me.

"How about right now?" I said back to him, and I reached down to pick up my guitar.

Simon cut his eyes at it. "Looks to me, you'd be better to take a gun."

"I'll take this," I said. "A gun wouldn't be enough for all who's out yonder."

"What if they hurt your guitar?" he inquired me next.

"They won't hurt it unless they kill me," I said, "and by then, it won't matter at all."

CHAPTER 16

When we got out into the yard outside the cabin, the night air felt so heavy it was like a quilt flung on you. Nair star winked in the hazy sky, there was just only the moon. That moon had a red glimmer, like as if it had been dipped in blood before it was hung up yonder.

Off in the direction toward Wolver, I could hear me a hum of something, a noise that might could be a big chance of voices or either just a stomping round. They were at their Sabbat doings, and that was a true word.

I looked up and down the road, then I scooted across it to the other side. Scrubby bushes grew up there, tall enough to hide a man who went amongst them. The air in there was heavier, foggier yet. Along back of me came Simon, sure-footed in the dark. I turned round to grin at him. Likely he couldn't see the grin, but he clapped me on the arm with his big, hard hand. Nor we didn't speak a word. It was no time and place to do talking. On we worked our way, toward where the racket was.

I should reckon it was more or less a mile through the brushy woods. We were out of sight of the road that might could have helped us take a direction. Up in the sky, as I've said, no stars—just that blood-dipped moon to help us guess the way. Meanwhile, the sounds got loud and louder, all mixed up of voices and some kind of music. I judged that to come from where the poor, torn-down old church house was. There would be a danger that we'd run into some watch-out guard party, and we were hard put to it to keep our feet quiet on the ground, to keep from a-rustling branches and twigs to either side. I thought to myself, maybe we'd make out a waiting guard before he made us out. What Simon thought about things I couldn't guess. But he came along. There was no puppy in Simon.

And then, light amongst the brush and trees up ahead where the noise was. I dropped myself almost double to sneak to where I could see from behind a big trunk. There I was, a-looking right into the churchyard at close quarters.

It was jam-pack full of people, with not just one but four–five fires a-burning red and luminous as the moon above. I had me no way to make out how many folks was there, but I'd say hundreds at least. That many in one place can make a right big crowd. And naked as jaybirds, their skins all a sweaty shine in the light of the fires, to the sound of the wildest music a man air heard in all his born days.

How they danced was thissaway: A circle of them moved in close order round the biggest of the fires amongst the tombstones. They went two and two, naked man and naked woman, and as they went they made a turn back to back, what the dance callers name do-si-do. The music wailed and whined and sort of flickered, a lonesome tune that seemed to be played in the cracks of the scale. It came from a knot of folks with instruments. One must have been a-blowing some kind of cornet or a horn like that, and he made it peal and whimper and reach out. There were fiddles, too, what they call the devil's instrument, a-playing all together a creepy harmony to that horn, and a drum, or likely more drums than one, that pounded out the beat for the dance.

Round and round stepped the naked folks in that circle. Sometimes a couple kissed one another. Outside the dancers was a bigger circle, drawn up to clap their hands in time to the music.

I was close enough where I was so that if I'd come out from behind my tree, I'd have been a-standing with them. I saw their backs, all naked too, and I made out little children in that outer circle. I said to myself, Tiphaine wants to catch her people young, all right.

A-looking past the tree and across the two circles, the moving one and the quiet one, I tried to spy out Tiphaine. But I didn't see her till all of a sudden the music quieted down and so did the dance. Those naked, sweaty folks stood where they stopped and sort of shuffled their bare feet. And I've got to vow, there wasn't a big many of them that looked pretty without their clothes. But I made out Tiphaine where she stood near that biggest fire.

She at least wasn't naked, she had on a pale robe that I figured was worked with lots of gold thread, it glistered so in the light. Her round, white arms were bare. She stood next to the Earth Mother statue—it must have taken a sight of hauling to get it out to that place. On her head she wore the horns I'd seen on her the other time. In front of her was set up their altar, a flat slab—likely a headstone hiked off its grave—across two chunks of rock. Behind Tiphaine stood three men. One must be Quill Norbury, in a long, dark gown with a hood. The other two, by the business suits they wore and I remembered, had to be the foreign men I'd seen with her, the two who'd come from their countries on business here.

Just as I picked Tiphaine out, she flung up her bare arms and whacked her hands together above her horned head. She called out something, I couldn't hear what, but the music completely quit and the dancers stood and stopped that movement with their feet. All that crowd harked at her, and so did I, and so did Simon.

"Rejoice, my people!" she bugled out so that the farthest of them could hear. "We seek and worship the one true wisdom!"

"AMIN!" the whole bunch yelled back, with one voice you'd think would carry for miles.

"Here in the dark, we know things forbidden to those who dwell in their own darkness!"

"AMIN!"

"Let us pledge one to the other in goblets of the miraculous wine!"

That time, no amins, the whole bunch just yelled and hollered. And I saw a bunch of girls run out, young naked girls with their hair a-flopping in the firelight, with armfuls of cups and great big crockery jugs, a-running here and yonder to fill the cups and pass them out. Another bunch came to serve the outer crowd where we stood just out of sight behind. I could almost have had me some of that wine by just a-holding my hand out for it.

Gentlemen, you should ought to have seen how those people grabbed onto the cups and guzzled, or more likely you're best off for not a-seeing it. For that was no right way to drink —slosh it down and hold out for more. I watched where Tiphaine and those men were, and it was poor Lute Baynor with her clothes off who had to fetch them wine. Lute looked like as if she shuddered, shrunk. One of the smart-suited foreign men drank and grinned to Tiphaine, and tried to put his arm round her. She twitched away from him, a-smiling back, and then he made a grab for Lute. She shrunk worse as she poured for him. Somebody started to sing in a screechy voice, and others joined in, and it went like this:

> "Cummer, go ye before, cummer, go ye;
> Gif ye not go before, cummer, let me!"

I'd heard the same song, a few nights back, the song that had been heard other times and often, at such meetings as this.

Those people drank, and they sort of drank two by two, the men with the women. They grinned on one another, and laughed to one another, and sort of wrestled together. I've heard tell of those who like to watch such a thing, but to me,

well, they aren't air great much for a spectator sport. I won't
go into the grapplings and rollings on the ground. Figure
them for yourselves if you want to. I heard Simon whisper, I
reckon he prayed. I couldn't say for certain, there was so
much almighty racket from all those others.

Simon and I watched, because there was naught else to do
right then. Time went on, seemed to me like quite a lot of
time. The people guzzled at their wine like as if it was their
only business in life. Might could have been, they didn't have
much chance at such wine, only at Sabbats. What made me
feel maddest was how the two foreign men pawed at poor
Lute Baynor. She didn't quite dare to fight them off, she just
only sort of struggled away from one of them, then the other.
I knew Tiphaine had promised her to them, and that would
be a-coming, I figured. But maybe not, maybe not. Maybe I'd
do something. I wondered what.

Finally Tiphaine smacked her hands again and hollered
out at the whole churchyard full of people. You can bet they
stopped their gabbling and laughing and listened.

"My people," she said out to them, and her voice could
sure enough carry. "This is our night of triumph. Here, with
us, are two new and powerful allies. They represent two
earthly governments of foreign lands, who now engage to support and advance our efforts in the world, among the legions
of the living!"

"AMIN!" came a-rolling back the response.

"The moment is now at hand," cried Tiphaine, "to deal
forever with an enemy to us, he who came unbidden!"

No amin to that, they all just stood and harked at her.

"John is his name," Tiphaine rolled forth. "He came,
proud and confident in his power. You know, all of you, that
I did my best to speak fair to him, to win him to a true light.
But he would not hear—he would not see reason!"

"AMIN!" it came out then.

"But now he lies a bound captive where he cannot win

free. Here with us we have what will be the end of him—destruction for him, triumph for us. Here!"

From somewhere she'd picked up what I knew was the wax image of me. She held it high in both hands, and all of them moaned and screeched.

"Here, for a sacrifice upon our sacred altar," Tiphaine was a-crying out to them, and she set the thing down. "Watch well, all of you, each of you. I will say a prayer, and then I will forever put an end to John and his works."

She flung her hands up to the murky sky.

"I'm a-going out," I said to Simon.

"I'll come with you."

"No, just me."

Because, if I couldn't do what must be done alone, the two of us couldn't do it.

I grabbed my guitar to me and struck the strings loud. I stepped out round the tree and up to where those people made that outer ring. They were close drawn, but I pushed right through and went with long steps amongst the others strewn here and there where the bushes and stones gave them room. I swept my strings and I sang the song that had more than once been a help to me in past days:

> Three holy kings, four holy saints,
> At heaven's high gate that stand,
> Speak out to bid all evil wait
> And stir no foot or hand . . .

Except for me, no foot or hand stirred.

A-walking and a-singing thattaway, I couldn't help but feel how alone I was amongst those hundreds. Nobody moved, nobody put out a hand to me. There was a little scuttling noise in some scrub, like something on four feet—a changeling, I made a guess. The folks, though, likely thought this was all a part of the show Tiphaine was a-putting on for them.

As for Tiphaine, she stood there in the firelight next to the altar, and the two foreigners had quit their fussing with Lute Baynor and looked at me, too. Lute slid off from them. Likewise, Quill Norbury had pulled back.

In the silence of that close air with the bloody moon above me, I made my stop right where Tiphaine stood. She was drawn up straight, her eyes made a shine in the light. Her face was pulled as tense as the head of a drum.

"John," she said. "What are you doing here?"

"I just came over to see what all the excitement was," I replied her, my thumb a-making a whisper of the silver strings.

She studied me and tried to understand. "But you were locked up tight," she said, like as if it was an accusation.

"I nair meant to let that stop me," I said to her. And if I made myself sound proud about it, I meant to.

"You're a dead man, John."

"Not me." I shook my head at her above the guitar. "You can't kill me." As I said that thing, I felt certain sure it was true.

"We'll see whether I can."

Up rose her hand, and I saw a flint point in it, one of the points she'd shown me on her table.

"You a-fixing to jab into that image of me?" I asked her. "Shoo, Tiphaine, that's naught but just a little old image." And I braced myself, in case she made a stab at me instead of that little, small, helpless-looking wax dummy.

"We'll see," she said again. She turned her tight face round. "Watch, all of you!" she screamed out.

Fast as a snake, she shot out her hand at the altar and brought the flint point down.

What happened then I sure enough didn't expect. I don't reckon I expected one thing or another, just that naught would happen when she jabbed at the image. But Tiphaine raised another scream, her loudest yet, like what an animal would make when it was struck where it lived. She stiffened up again, whirled halfway round, and then, right that moment, she slammed down to the ground. There she lay, with no more movement than the wax image.

They all of them let out a holler then. It would have deafened you, you'd expect. I looked at the altar. The point was stuck in the wax breast, and I reached and picked it out. Again I looked at where Tiphaine had fallen. Still she lay as a stone, and she seemed smaller than air I'd seen her. I've been next to too many dead bodies not to know one when I see it.

"She's gone," I said out loud. "Past help."

Lute Baynor was beside me. She'd pulled some sort of checked cloth round her nakedness, something like a drape or tablecloth. The firelight made her face flicker. She looked down, too.

"Dead!" she wailed. "Tiphaine's dead, she's dead!"

"Ooooh," said someone in the crowd, nearby.

"What must we do?" said another.

The two foreigners went on a run through the tombstones and brush, like as if dogs were after them. Quill Norbury was gone out of sight.

"Wh-what?" blubbered Ottom Orcutt, a-coming to me. Hair was bunchy on his big naked chest. The whites of his eyes shone like on a scared horse. "What happened?"

"Tiphaine died, not me," I said, surprised at how quiet I sounded. "Her magic didn't work on me. But she'd called for a dead sacrifice. I reckon, it bounced back on her."

He hunkered down and goggled at Tiphaine.

"Yes, she's—" He sort of choked on the words. "Snatched away—we'll be snatched away, too." He looked up at me. "Do something, John, save us!"

"Save us," moaned somebody else, from amongst where they all bunched and bobbed together, scared silly.

"We did wrong," Ottom whimpered.

"We were fools," put in another. "Trusted her—"

"Trusted Tiphaine!"

"She's gone," I said again.

"John," Ottom begged to me. "You were right, she was wrong—save us—"

"Save us!" yammered a bunch of them together.

I flung up my hands, with the guitar in them.

"Folks, hear me," I said, the loudest I could. "I'm no preacher man, myself, but you need one. I can give you one. Simon Latchney—let him talk to you!"

How they moaned and sobbed. Simon came, quick as he could, there amongst where they all knelt and cried, near about scared out of their bare hides. He came to where I stood, by that altar they'd made, and Tiphaine down under it.

"Friends," his voice pealed out. "You who are weary and heavy-laden, remember that the good Lord in heaven doesn't desire the death of a sinner. Let me say words to comfort you, out of the holy Book of Psalms."

They'd quieted to hear him. He looked round, and then:

> If I take the wings of the morning, and dwell in the uttermost parts of the sea; even there shall thy hand lead me, and thy right hand shall hold me.

As he spoke, the heavy went out of the air. The sky cleared in a wink of time, like as if a veil had been snatched off of it. The moon came out, sweet and pale. And I saw all the stars, a-shining down on us in their faithful beauty.